ETERNAL LOVE

LINDA FAUSNET

To all of my readers, both old and new, for coming with me on my writer journey, which often strays from the usual path. When you don't "write-to-market", you win some and you lose some. Heartfelt thanks for making my oddball ghost stories a winner.

My books contain steamy sex, bad words, and human beings of all sorts, include gay people. If you're not a fan of those things, you may want to stop reading now. If you're cool with that stuff, come take my hand and join me on this journey...

This book is a work of fiction. References to real people, events, establishments, organizations, or locales are intended only to provide a sense of authenticity and are used fictitiously. All other characters, and all incidents and dialogue, are drawn from the author's imagination and are not to be construed as real.

Published by Wannabe Pride 2020

Editing by Linda Hill

Cover Design by Chuck DeKett

FIRST EDITION.

Library of Congress Control Number: 2020902606

ISBN: 978-1-944043-53-7

❦ Created with Vellum

1

Some people were naturally sensitive to the presence of ghosts. They felt it when a spirit was nearby. They might look up uncertainly and perhaps shiver, disturbed by the feeling they were being watched.

Gregory Markham was not one of those people.

He never noticed spirits. Gregory was utterly unaware of the female spirit who visited him almost daily as he worked in Hay's Cabinetmaker's Shop in Colonial Williamsburg, Virginia. A skilled carpenter and an expert in 18th-century woodworking, he spent his days crafting wooden tables, chairs, harpsichords, and various other items.

Visitors came from all over the world to tour Williamsburg's historical buildings and to visit with guides like Gregory who dressed in 18th-century clothing and demonstrated typical 1700s activities. Guests would usually find him hunched over his current woodworking project, his dark brown hair hanging down and his face scrunched with concentration. While he toiled on his woodworking and spoke to tourists that visited his shop daily, Gregory hadn't a clue that his shop was haunted.

Rebekah Jennings died in 1762 at the tender age of twenty, but her spirit had remained earthbound. In more than two hundred and fifty years, she had never encountered a man as perfectly lovely as Gregory. Invisible, she would walk through the shop, observing visitors but mostly focusing on him. He typically worked at least five days a week on a rotating schedule, and she had visited him on many of his working days since he was hired six months ago. She'd stand nearby, admiring his big, skillful hands as they transformed blocks of wood into exquisite works of art. She'd gaze fondly at his dark brown eyes and impossibly long lashes. His sturdy, manly build in his dark trousers and flowing, white shirt with the first few buttons undone stirred feelings of desire she'd never known in life. Gregory wasn't simply a handsome man who could work well with his hands. He had a gentle and friendly disposition, especially with the children who visited his shop. Not only had he crafted the ornately carved harpsichord on display in the shop, he was also an incredibly talented musician. He never looked more handsome than when he played the harpsichord. His eyes flashed and his hands danced across the keys with a passionate flourish.

He knew many 18th-century tunes, but he also knew how to play lots of modern ones. Rebekah was familiar with current pop culture, including songs, television shows, and movies. She'd been around for hundreds of years, unable to do much more than observe the world around her, so she was always aware of current trends. When tourists came into his shop wearing T-shirts with band names on them, Gregory would frequently play a song from that musical group. An adorable red-headed teenager had come into the shop this morning, sporting a Led Zeppelin shirt. After complimenting the lad on his good taste in classic rock,

Gregory played a few bars of "Stairway to Heaven." The kid grinned slightly, which was a huge display of emotion coming from a teenager.

Gregory often paused his work when little children came to visit his shop, taking care to give them special attention. For the little guys, he would play "If You're Happy and You Know It" or "The Wheels on the Bus" on the harpsichord. Rebekah loved to watch his sweet brown eyes light up with joy at the sound of a child's giggle.

He seemed aware of the effect he had on the teenage girls who frequently stared at him, and he often smiled warmly at them, being sure to make eye contact. Of the many things Rebekah admired about him, his way of making everyone feel special was near the top of the list.

Oh, how she loved him.

Now, Rebekah's phantom heart skipped a beat when Gregory looked up as several tourists entered the shop. He couldn't see her, of course, but it was pleasant to imagine he was looking right at her. She tore her gaze from him to watch the family of four as they explored the place. Though she no longer had her sense of smell, Rebekah knew—remembered, actually—what the shop smelled like. The scent of sawdust and fresh cut wood permeated the air. Not all the current buildings in Colonial Williamsburg existed in the 1700s, but Hay's was one of the original buildings, restored to look much as it did when Rebekah was a girl. She had visited the shop with her father to pick up freshly carved furniture for Jennings Tavern, which had been owned by her family.

Rebekah watched the tourist family—parents and two little boys—as they looked at the woodworks on display. Upon entering the cabinetmaker's shop, tourists walked through a hallway where they were treated to a display of numerous finely crafted items, including a grandfather clock, a desk, several chairs, and even a coffin that leaned up against the wall. There were several windows on both sides of the hallway, providing natural light and eliminating the need for modern electric lights that might spoil the historical atmosphere. The hallway led to a large room, which was the main area of the shop where Gregory worked. His work bench was to the right of the doorway from the hall and facing the exit door of the building. From this spot, he could hear when the back door of the building opened and people came in, and he could see when they exited to the outside. The shop room was filled with wooden pieces in various shapes, cuts, and sizes resting on long wooden tables. The walls were decorated with hanging tools: everything from large saws to smaller tools used to create intricate designs.

Though currently invisible, Rebekah had the ability to appear whenever she wished. She frequently walked down the streets of Colonial Williamsburg fully visible. When people saw the young woman with flowing light brown hair and gray eyes, they had no idea she was a dead woman. That was the advantage of having died near an area that was now populated with modern-day workers dressed in clothing from more than two centuries ago. No one batted an eye when they saw Rebekah, as she blended in almost perfectly in this historical district. She also frequently spoke to the tourists, and they were none the wiser. So long as no one tried to touch her, she could easily pass for a living, breathing woman. As a spirit, she retained her sense of sight and hearing but had lost her sense of touch and taste as well as smell.

Of course, all her feelings and memories from her long existence remained. Memories of when she was alive and of everything she had seen and heard over the last two and half centuries. In all that time, Rebekah had had no choice but to keep within a ten-mile radius of where she had lived and died. It was impossible to travel any further. She had tried many times. Once she got past a certain point, she simply disappeared and then reappeared at her starting point. She was forced to remain in this limited area until she figured out a way to cross over to the other side. She'd seen it happen to dozens of spirits over the years, but it felt like her own time would never come.

Perhaps that was as it should be. Rebekah knew she didn't deserve to go to Heaven, so here she would stay.

Even so, she had felt touches of God's mercy during her lonely existence. Whenever she felt weary of simply existing, she could vanish for a while. It was a sort of sleep for ghosts, the ability to vanish for as long as they wished, for a night or even for years at a time. Being constantly conscious, day and night for decades, would drive anyone mad. Vanishing provided a much-needed reprieve.

Rebekah's gaze returned to Gregory, whose presence was more evidence of God's kindness. Watching him brought her the greatest joy she'd experienced since her death. In life, she'd never known the love of a man, physically or otherwise. Her parents had been genuinely worried she would wind up a spinster. She'd had one offer of marriage, but she'd turned the man down. Rebekah was a romantic and believed deeply in love. She adored Shakespeare's love sonnets and stories, and she had dreamed of meeting a handsome man who would sweep her off her feet.

Too late for that now. Much, much too late. Even so, being near Gregory provided her with endless romantic daydreams. She spent hours imagining what it would be like to just speak with him. To have him *see* her. He smiled at everyone, so she knew he would smile at her if she caught his eye. But what would he think of her? Would he think her plain? Pretty? In life, she'd been told she was beautiful. Still, it was hard to know if it was true or if people were simply being kind. She'd died wearing a plain white cotton dress with a faint pink floral pattern, so that was her outfit for eternity. Had she known, perhaps she would have worn a fancier gown that day.

Though she'd fantasized about a meeting with Gregory, she'd never let him see her. What would be the point? In her imagination, he gazed upon her tenderly and called her beautiful. In reality, he would probably give her a polite smile, believing she was a fellow Colonial Williamsburg co-worker. No. It was best to keep her relationship with Gregory safe and secure in her mind. There, everything was perfect between them. She wasn't an ugly, dead thing. Rebekah was as alive as he was, and they were madly in love. Engaged to be married with their whole lives ahead of them.

Rebekah couldn't help daydreaming about what a gentle lover he would be. Knowing she was a maiden, he would be tender and go slowly.

Immersed in her fantasies, Rebekah snapped back to reality when she heard the grandfather clock strike 5pm. Closing time for the historical buildings in Colonial Williamsburg. Though both the general public and tourists who had paid for passes that permitted them to enter the buildings were free to roam the streets of the historic district after hours, all the workers would now be heading home. She would have to wait until tomorrow to see Gregory again.

When the tourists left Hay's Cabinetmaker's Shop, Rebekah knew she should leave, too. She was always respectful of Gregory's privacy, trying not to watch him when he was alone. It was different when there were tourists around and when Ben was there. Ben was an older, retired gentleman who worked on a part-time basis in the shop. Still, she always struggled to leave Gregory at the end of the day. She usually lingered as she watched him put away his woodworking tools for the night. He often sang softly to himself as he wrapped up his work, which made Rebekah smile. He seemed passionate about music in all its forms, as was she.

Her family had always told her she had a pretty singing voice. Singing had been a great passion of hers when she was alive. She sang constantly in life. She sang as she worked, sang for her family, and sang even just for herself. Singing had always been an emotional release for her.

Rebekah hadn't sung a note since her death.

She didn't deserve the joy and pleasure singing gave her.

Feeling that familiar sense of loneliness creep in, she turned and drifted out of the cabinetmaker's shop. Fortunately, she knew he was scheduled to work tomorrow, so she wouldn't have to wait long to see him again.

As always, she wondered where Gregory would go after work. For all she knew, he had a girlfriend. It was too painful to think about, so she rarely did. Rebekah wanted him to be happy. Even so, if he had a woman in his life, she really didn't want to know. She knew it was silly of her to feel that way.

Gregory was a good, honest, and kind gentleman.

Even if she had been alive, she would never have been worthy of him.

2

Gregory smiled warmly at the shy teenage girl who was awkwardly doing that looking-but-trying-not-to-look thing at him. He got that a lot, and he realized that girls found him at least moderately attractive for some reason. That was why he always made sure to smile back at them. He remembered all too well how it felt to be that age. He recalled that time a troupe of twenty-something actors had visited his high school to perform Shakespeare's "Twelfth Night." Gregory's teenaged heart had been captured by the actress playing Viola. Between her beauty and her acting talent, he was quite taken with her. During the question and answer in his classroom after the performance, he'd been far too shy to speak up. But the woman had caught his eye and smiled warmly. At fifteen years old, he knew it didn't mean anything. Still, it made him feel like a million bucks. If he could make somebody else feel that way, he would. Any chance he got. Besides, he was quite fond of kids of all ages, even sulky teenagers.

The teenage girl and her family wandered around the shop and then headed out. The back door opened again, and Gregory heard a new group of tourists enter. Now that it was springtime, the crowds were getting heavier and there was a steadier stream of guests to visit his shop. He turned his attention back to the card table he was crafting as the people came into the room after exploring the hallway displays.

He enjoyed interacting with tourists, and he loved woodworking. Sometimes he could hardly believe he got paid to do both. Crafting beautiful things out of wood was a form of therapy. His life had been quite turbulent over the last year, and working here brought a sense of peace. Only music could top woodworking for its calming effect, which was why he loved the shop's harpsichord. He had made a large portion of it with his own two hands, with the help of other craftsmen. It had taken months to build, and playing it brought him a sense of calm and happiness.

Moving to Colonial Williamsburg had definitely been the right thing to do, no matter what his family thought. He'd been here for six months, and he felt slightly better with each passing day. The rest of his family was still in Florida. His parents, his brother, and his sister. And his ex-wife.

He'd never expected to be divorced at the age of twenty-eight, but here he was. More than anything, he had wanted to be married and raise a happy family. He supposed if he was lucky that still might happen, but it wouldn't be any time soon.

Gregory had desperately needed to get away from the heartache and pain of his marriage ending. He'd always been a student of history, and working at Colonial Williamsburg felt like stepping back in time. The curators of the historical district made a conscientious effort to preserve the colonial feel, forbidding modern vehicles on the main street during the day. Instead, the clop-trop of horses and carriages could be heard outside. The atmosphere was quiet and calm, despite the presence of hundreds of tourists visiting each day. Music frequently filled the air with the sound of tin whistles being played beautifully by Williamsburg employees and being played badly, yet adorably, by little kids whose parents probably regretted their gift shop purchase. Soldiers marched down Duke of Gloucester Street playing fifes and drums, which was always a crowd-pleaser.

The day had passed quickly, as it usually did on Fridays when the place was busy. It was well past 5pm, and Gregory knew he should leave. He was never in a hurry to go home at the end of the day. After all, there was nobody to go home to. He'd made a few acquaintances here, but they were mostly co-workers who had their own friends to hang out with on the weekends. Gregory liked his apartment well enough, but it was only temporary until he figured out where he wanted to live permanently. Though he hoped to buy a home someday, he worried it would feel especially lonely to putter around in a house all alone.

His stomach growled, but he was too engrossed in finishing the ornate foot of the card table to stop now. Humming to himself, he used a small paring chisel to carve details on the claw and the ball of the foot of the table leg. The project was turning out well and he was eager to see the finished product. It was so satisfying to make something sturdy and beautiful with your own two hands.

Feeling slightly dizzy, Gregory knew damned well it was past time to stop. Sometimes, when he was really in the zone, it was too difficult to tear himself away.

Just a few more minutes, he told himself. He finished the toe of the table leg.

Wow.

He couldn't help being impressed with his own work. Pleased with what he had accomplished for the day, he finally stood up to leave.

And nearly fell to the floor.

A severe wave of dizziness crashed over him.

"Oh, shit," he mumbled, grabbing onto the carpentry table to try to steady himself. Gregory's hands, which had been so steady moments before, shook violently. Opening his eyes wide, he tried to focus, but the entire room was suddenly blurry.

Oh God. I'm in trouble.

Then everything went black.

3

"Gregory!" Rebekah shouted as she watched him collapse to the floor. Of course, he couldn't hear her because she was still invisible.

She understood at once what was happening to him. She had overheard him talking about having diabetes, and she knew he was going into diabetic shock. She'd seen him have minor episodes before, but nothing this bad. He was in serious danger, and the only person around to help was a woman who was unable to touch anything.

She tried to focus and stem her rising panic. Gregory lay still, eyes closed, and Rebekah knew she had to rouse him somehow. She drifted into the hallway that led to the shop. Then she turned herself visible and shouted his name with all her might.

"Gregory! Wake up! Gregory!"

Peering into the shop area, Rebekah saw his eyes open wide. She watched as he glanced around the shop to see who had shouted his name. He blinked rapidly, likely trying to make sense of where he was and what was happening. Groaning, he managed to stagger to his feet. She disappeared again so she could be by his side without frightening him to death.

Slowly, carefully, Gregory made his way over to a large wooden chest against the wall.

"That's it, darling. Slow and steady. You can do this," Rebekah coached. Though he couldn't hear her, it made her feel better to speak to him in a soothing voice. Perhaps on a sub-conscious level, he could feel her loving presence guiding him. "You've almost got it."

He needed sugar in his bloodstream immediately because he had waited too long to eat. Rebekah knew he kept sugar tablets on top of the wooden chest. She'd seen him reach for them before, usually when he seemed to be feeling only slightly dizzy. His appearance, pale and shaky, terrified her now. She knew the next few moments were critical. If he didn't get sugar into his system right away, he could slip into a coma.

He could *die*.

Hands shaking violently, Gregory grasped the cardboard package of pills.

"That's it, that's it now. You're almost there," Rebekah told him.

He struggled with the package, unable to get the blister pack open.

Please oh please.

She watched him helplessly, horrified that there was nothing she could do but hope and pray he could open the package.

Frustrated and clearly afraid, Gregory clawed at it, despite his dizziness. Finally, he managed to rip it open. But the package flew from his hands and fell underneath the dresser. And out of his reach.

"No!" Rebekah screamed. Terror consumed her.

As a spirit, she was able to slip through the wooden chest and see behind it. She found the package far underneath the chest. The only way to grab it would be to move the heavy piece of furniture away from the wall. Nearly incapacitated, Gregory couldn't possibly move it. Ghosts had the ability to grasp small items or move furniture, but it required a tremendous amount of skill and concentration. Besides, usually angry ghosts had the strength to move objects. The more consumed with rage they were, the more power they had. And the more damage they could do. Rebekah was an utter emotional wreck—she couldn't possibly gather enough strength to grab the package, let alone move the chest.

Defeated, Gregory groaned and staggered backward. He let out a deep sigh and slowly sank to the floor. Like he was giving up.

Frozen with fear, Rebekah's eyes darted around the room. Should she run and get help?

No. There wasn't time. He could be dead by the time she returned. Gregory could barely keep his eyes open. He might slip into a coma at any moment.

And never wake up.

"Oh, sweet Gregory. I don't know what to do!" she wailed out loud. "I don't know what to—"

The answer suddenly came to her. She might be able to save him, but he had to be able to stand up again. Shouting his name might not be enough.

She had to scare him.

Still invisible, she drifted in front of him. She reached down and touched his face, knowing the sensation would feel quite cold against his cheek. Gregory's eyes opened the tiniest bit, and she seized her opportunity.

She faded into view right in front of him.

Gregory's eyes shot open wide with horror. Seeing a ghost was enough to startle him back to consciousness, if only for a moment.

He let out a strangled, terrified cry. Rebekah tried to ignore the stabbing pain in her heart as the man she loved looked at her with sheer terror. This was what she was going for, of course, but he would never think her beautiful now. He probably thought she was a hideous monster, a ghoul.

Gregory's eyes widened even more, and he tried to scoot backwards and away from her.

"It's all right. I'm not going to hurt you. I'm here to help you," Rebekah said in a voice she hoped was both commanding and soothing. If she frightened him too much, he might pass out from fear, and all would be lost.

"Ah ... ah ... ah," Gregory croaked in fear, still backing away.

There wasn't another second to lose.

"Gregory Markham, you listen to me!" she commanded.

He blinked, clearly stunned and confused that she knew his name.

"Gregory," she continued firmly, meeting his eye and willing him to focus on her words. "I know you're sick. I know you need those tablets that you can't reach."

He stared, looking more confused than frightened.

"The package of pills landed right in the middle underneath the wood chest near the wall, and I know you don't have the strength right now to move something so heavy. But it's all right. I can help you," she said, her tone much gentler than before. She relished the glimmer of hope she saw in his eyes. Although he was afraid, he must have known she was his last hope. He might not understand what was going on, but he had little to lose by listening to her.

"Ben left half a bottle of cola next to his carpentry table,"

Rebekah said. Carefully, she walked rather than floated over to the wooden table.

She gestured toward the floor where the plastic half-bottle of Coca-Cola still rested. Gregory's eyes followed her gesture, and his eyes filled with hope when he saw the sugary drink. He glanced hesitantly up at Rebekah, and she realized he must be afraid to approach the bottle with a dead woman standing near it.

Again, she walked slowly, carefully away from the table. Had Gregory not seen her appear out of nowhere, he never would have known she was dead. But he did know, and there was no going back. Still, she wasn't sorry. Scaring him had worked, and that was what mattered.

From a safe distance in the hallway, Rebekah said gently, "It's all right. Don't be afraid, but don't dawdle. Get the drink, Gregory!"

He began crawling on his hands and knees toward the soda bottle. Grasping it, he struggled with the cap. At last, he got the bottle open and managed to gulp down the drink.

"Oh, thank God!" she called out. Her voice startled him. It might take a few minutes for his system to absorb the sugar, but hopefully he would be okay now.

Shaky and pale, Gregory turned his head toward Rebekah, eying her with confusion. In his dizzy state, it must have been hard enough to think straight without being visited by a ghost.

"Everything is going to be just fine. Just stay right there, and I'll get you some help, all right?"

He squinted at her, understandably looking quite perplexed, but he nodded.

Not wishing to frighten him further, Rebekah walked briskly through the hallway and toward the door instead of floating there. She winced when she reached the door. She couldn't open it. There was no way out for her but *through* it. Hoping he wasn't watching her, she floated right through it.

She tried to ignore the sharp gasp she heard from behind her as she left.

Once outside, Rebekah rushed up the hill and headed straight toward Duke of Gloucester Street where there were bound to be tourists still around. Though all the Colonial Williamsburg official buildings were closed for the day, some of the shops were open, as were many of the taverns for dinner.

Rebekah rushed up to the first group of tourists she found—a man and a woman walking with two small boys.

"Please, I need help! There's a man over there going into diabetic shock!" Rebekah said, eyes wide.

The man glanced at his wife.

"On it," she said firmly. "It's all right, ma'am. I'm an EMT. I can help."

The woman had short, dark black hair and kind but somewhat piercing blue eyes. Rebekah already felt better.

"Oh, thank goodness. He was able to get to some sugar just now. I found some cola for him, but he's still a little dizzy and he might need medical attention."

"Yes, I'm calling in from the Colonial Williamsburg historic district," the man said into his cell phone. "I've got a man here with a possible diabetic emergency." The man turned to Rebekah. "What building?"

"Hay's Cabinetmaker's Shop. Just off Nicholson Street," she replied.

As the man repeated the information into the phone, the woman reached for Rebekah's arm.

Rebekah jumped away before the woman's hand went right through her body.

"Sorry! I'm just a little jumpy," Rebekah said.

"It's okay," the woman said. "Just lead me to the building and the paramedics will meet us there."

Rebekah nodded, and they headed back to the shop.

"I'm Alicia, by the way."

"Thank you so much for your help, Alicia."

When they got to the back door of the shop, Rebekah gestured for Alicia to go first. Fortunately, Gregory hadn't locked the door. Sometimes he left it unlocked when he got absorbed in his work. Alicia opened the door and entered, and Rebekah followed her.

"In that back room there," Rebekah said, gesturing toward the shop room.

They found Gregory lying on the floor with his eyes closed.

Oh God, he didn't make it.

He's gone.

Just as Rebekah was about to let out a cry of sheer grief, she saw his chest move with his breathing.

"Sir?" Alicia called out to him.

"His name is Gregory. Gregory Markham," Rebekah told her.

"Mr. Markham?" Alicia said as she knelt beside him.

Gregory's eyes fluttered open.

"It's all right," Alicia said in a calm but firm voice. "You've had a bit of an emergency I hear, but you're gonna be okay. My name's Alicia, and I'm an EMT. You're in good hands. I promise."

Gregory's eyes seemed much more focused now, and the color had returned to his face.

As much as it pained her, Rebekah knew she had to leave before he said anything to Alicia about her appearing from nowhere.

She heard sirens in the distance. Gregory had help now, and he was going to be okay.

With one last look at him, she turned invisible and quietly slipped out.

4

od, what an idiot I am.

Gregory lay in bed the next morning thinking about how he had damn near killed himself. He'd been diagnosed with diabetes when he was fifteen years old, so he knew how to manage the disease. He couldn't believe how stupid he'd been to take such a risk, just to finish a table leg. Thank God the EMT lady had shown up.

The details of yesterday's events were still rather hazy. He'd been working alone when he passed out, and it was too late in the evening for tourists to come into the shop. So how had that Alicia woman known he needed help? Perhaps Ben had stopped by after work and found him unconscious.

Gregory had been so out of it, he'd been hallucinating. He'd thought he'd seen the ghost of some 18th-century woman.

A chill went through him when he thought about it.

He'd heard her voice, and she smelled like flowers. Fairly vivid details for a hallucination, but it was the only explanation. The apparition couldn't possibly have been real.

No. It was definitely a hallucination. The room had spun, and he'd barely seen straight. Naturally, his mind would play tricks on him.

But what about the bottle of soda?

Gregory hadn't noticed Ben drinking it last time he'd worked with him. He'd had no idea there was a half-empty Coke bottle on the floor, hidden among discarded pieces of wood and covered in sawdust.

I only found the bottle because the woman told me it was there.

But that wasn't possible ... was it? Was she an angel sent to help him?

He laughed out loud as he threw the covers off the bed. There was no way he saw an angel, or a ghost, or anything like that. He must have seen the bottle at some point and remembered where it was. Or perhaps he stumbled across it when he was crawling around the floor.

No question about it. The ghostly woman had simply been a figment of his imagination brought on by his condition. All that mattered was he'd found the Coke bottle, and he was okay. Gregory couldn't help thinking about what could have happened yesterday. If Ben hadn't left his drink on the floor, Gregory might have been found dead this morning. He felt a sharp, physical ache in his chest when he imagined someone calling his parents to tell them their son had died.

Gregory vowed to never, ever be so damned stupid again.

∼

Ben was already in the shop when Gregory arrived, his stout frame seated at his worktable. With his gray beard and friendly manner, he resembled Santa Claus hard at work in his toy shop. He frequently worked on Saturdays because tourist traffic was heavier, and Gregory needed the help.

"Hey, are you okay?" Ben asked, looking up from his carpentry table when Gregory walked in. "I heard what happened."

Okay. So, Ben wasn't the one who went and got help for me.

"Oh yeah, I'm fine. Really. Good thing you're such a slob," Gregory said with a grin. "It was your leftover soda that saved my life."

"Yeah?" Ben said, eyes wide. "What about your pills?"

"I dropped 'em when I was trying to open the package," Gregory said. "Which reminds me ..."

He walked over to the big wooden chest. Grasping it with both hands, he pulled the large piece of furniture away from the wall to retrieve his glucose tablets. He found them on the floor, smack dab in the middle of where the chest had been.

Exactly where the ghostly woman had said they had landed.

Gregory stared at the package for a moment.

"You all right?" Ben asked. "You look a little pale."

Still staring at the pills, he responded, "Yeah, I'm fine."

I'm just losing my mind, that's all.

Gregory picked up the package of pills and ripped it apart where it was perforated. He put half of them on top of the chest, then pushed the chest back against the wall. He slipped the other sheet of pills into a drawer in his carpentry table. After what happened yesterday, he was tempted to place packets of sugar all over the damned shop, just to be safe.

"Good thing that tourist lady happened to be a medic, huh?" Ben said, shaking his head.

"Yeah. How did she know I was here?"

"No idea. I'm just glad she got to ya in time."

Gregory turned over the events in his mind. It occurred to him that he didn't recall locking the door at 5pm like he was supposed to. He'd gotten so wrapped up in his table project, he'd simply forgotten. The tourist woman had probably just wandered in off the street, not realizing the building was supposed to be closed for the night.

Yes. That was the only explanation that made sense.

Gregory busied himself with his work. Since it was a warm spring day, lots of tourists came through the shop. He alternated between getting engrossed in his work on the card table and speaking with visitors. One man was a carpenter by trade and was fascinated by Gregory's craftsmanship. They had an absorbing conversation, and the morning flew by rather quickly.

"Why don't you go take your lunch break now?" Ben said at the stroke of noon. He'd been eying Gregory with concern all morning.

"Okay. I won't be too long."

"Take your time," Ben said. He reminded Gregory of his father, the way he looked out for him.

Gregory stepped outside and paused on the small wooden bridge covering the stream that ran under the building. He always enjoyed the peaceful atmosphere behind the shop. The cluster of trees provided shade on a sunny day, and the trickling sound of the water rushing over the stones was soothing. On slow days, he frequently stepped outside to breathe in the fresh air and recharge. The area also afforded him some privacy to prick his finger to check his sugar before he took some pre-lunch insulin. Not wanting to gross anybody out, he always made sure there were no tourists around before doing so.

It took about fifteen minutes for the insulin to kick in, which gave him just enough time to stroll down the street and find a shady place to sit so he could eat. He went to one of his favorite spots underneath a tree across the street from Market Square. There was heavy foot traffic all around. He enjoyed people-watching; the spot was perfect.

"Mr. Markham!" called a friendly female voice.

Alicia walked toward him with her husband and two little boys.

"Hey," Gregory called with a friendly wave.

The boys giggled and chased each other, making Gregory laugh.

"How are you feeling?" she asked, keeping an eye on the boys.

"Better. Much better. Thanks again for your help. I really appreciate it. Sorry to put a damper on your family vacation."

"Not at all. Had the outcome been different, now *that* would put a damper on things. But you're lookin' good. Healthy. That's all that matters."

"Thanks to you."

Alicia shrugged. "Not really. I didn't have to do much. Your friend was the one who found that soda pop for you."

Gregory's blood suddenly ran cold.

"Friend? What friend?"

"That woman who came running up asking for help. She told me she got you some cola, but she still wanted somebody to check on you to make sure you were all right. She was so upset, I thought she might have been your wife or girlfriend. But then she disappeared."

"D—d—disappeared?"

"Yeah. She left while I was taking care of you. Didn't catch her name before she took off. Oh well. I'm just glad you're okay."

"Thanks again," Gregory managed to say.

"Hey! No hitting!" Alicia admonished her kids. Laughing, she said, "Sorry, gotta go."

"Okay. Have fun today," he said.

Alicia and her husband offered friendly waves, then they were off to wrangle their kids.

Feeling dazed, Gregory rested his back against the tree.

The woman was real.

He tried to wrap his mind around what Alicia had just told him. There really had been a woman there yesterday, and she had led him to what he needed to survive.

Gregory reasoned that it was hardly unusual to see a woman dressed in 18th-century garb around here. Lots of people wore it. He was dressed that way right now. He clearly hadn't imagined the woman's existence, but he *must* have imagined her appearing out of thin air right in front of him.

Not surprising, considering I was barely conscious.

Yes. That must have been what happened. Some woman who worked for Colonial Williamsburg had come into the shop for some reason and found him in need of medical assistance.

Still, Gregory couldn't shake the vision of her *appearing* to him.

Not only that, but he'd seen her walk *through the door* on her way out.

And there was one more thing.

She knew his name. Gregory clearly remembered her calling him by his full name.

Gregory Markham, you listen to me!

Not only did she know his name, but she knew he had diabetes. She knew exactly where his pills had fallen, and she knew Ben had left a soda bottle on the floor.

A fresh wave of dizziness overcame him; a mixture of fear and the fact that he still hadn't eaten anything. He'd lost his appetite, but he forced himself to eat his sandwich anyway.

Though it was scary to face the prospect that he might have been visited by a ghost yesterday, his fear began to subside the more he thought about her.

Whoever or whatever she was, had she not been there, he most likely would have slipped into a coma and died. Some poor, unsuspecting tourists would have found him dead this morning. Gregory found himself thinking of his parents again, getting the phone call that every parent dreads.

We're so sorry to inform you that—

Gregory shook his head as if to ward off those terrible thoughts. Instead of dwelling on what could have happened, he thought about the woman with the long brown hair. She had been so concerned about him. He knew he'd never forget the fear he saw in her soft, caring gray eyes, nor the kindness and sweet relief on her face after he swallowed the sugary drink.

There was no question about it. The woman had saved his life. And he never got to thank her.

For some reason, this woman was still roaming around Williamsburg after her death.

Gregory began to wonder if perhaps there was some way to find her.

5

Rebekah had decided she would no longer visit Gregory. After briefly going to the cabinetmaker's shop to make sure he was all right, she left quickly. Ben was with him, and Gregory looked healthy. Healthy and perfect. Unable to bear the idea of hearing what Gregory might say about her, she had fled.

I could swear I saw this creepy dead lady. She walked right through the door. It was horrible. Monstrous.

Rebekah knew she would never be able to erase Gregory's terrorized expression from her mind. Her heart ached as she recalled the way he had backed away from her, trying to escape her nightmarish presence. The way he'd been afraid to go near the carpentry table where she stood, even though he knew he could die if he didn't get to the bottle right away.

In her fantasies, she had always dreamed of Gregory gazing upon her admiringly. Now he knew she was a ghost. A disgusting, dead thing. Something to fear.

Repulsed. He was *repulsed* by her.

Consumed with sorrow and self-pity, she had spent all

night weeping. Her brief time with Gregory was over. She could never go back to see him now. Not without remembering him recoiling in terror. Her existence would be lonelier than ever before.

And yet, it had all been worth it to save his precious life. Of course it had. Rebekah would do anything to protect him. Perhaps it was destiny for her to be near him when he needed her, and now she was destined to bear the pain of his loss.

After what she had done in life, it was the punishment she deserved.

∾

GREGORY WONDERED if the woman was in the shop with him. She had appeared out of nowhere yesterday. For all he knew, she was here even though he couldn't see her. Were there others, he wondered? Maybe ghosts were all over the place.

He shuddered at the creepy thought.

Still, the woman hadn't seemed creepy. She had saved his life, after all. Strangely, if Gregory hadn't seen her appear out of thin air, he probably would have taken her for a living person. He recalled the way she walked, the way she spoke. It had all seemed normal. If he'd seen her walking down Duke of Gloucester Street, he would have assumed she worked for Colonial Williamsburg. The only difference was the way she wore her hair. All the costumed women around here usually wore their hair under bonnets or hats, as was the custom for the 18th century. The ghostly woman's hair flowed down her back instead. Maybe she died in her sleep and she wasn't wearing a bonnet.

Gregory shuddered again, thinking about the woman's death. Dead. Dead. This lady was *dead,* yet she still roamed the streets of Colonial Williamsburg. Naturally, people told ghost stories around here all the time, but he had never believed them.

Until now.

As it was just past 5pm, Ben started packing up his stuff to leave for the night. Gregory watched as he picked up his almost-empty paper cup of lemonade, paused slightly, then set it down again.

"Maybe I'll just leave this here," Ben muttered.

Gregory chuckled.

"It's okay, Ben. Throw it out. I've got pills in my table drawer now."

Ben laughed and picked up his trash. "Okay, then."

"Have a good night."

Ben shot him a worried look. "I'm not crazy about leaving you alone."

Maybe I'm not alone.

"I'll be fine. I'm right behind ya. I promise. Just need five more minutes."

Ben nodded, his brow still furrowed with concern, but he headed out.

After Ben closed the door, Gregory glanced around.

Was the ghost woman here now?

Yesterday, she'd seen what was happening to him and probably felt she had no choice but to step in and help him by showing herself. If she was here now, maybe she was deliberately staying hidden.

Slowly, Gregory stood up from his carpentry table. He looked around, acutely aware of the silence. A sliver of fear went through him. He'd never really been afraid of ghosts before, but that was mainly because he hadn't believed in them. That had all changed.

"Hello?" he called out. His voice was met with silence. Gregory held still for a moment, listening carefully. Nothing.

"Are you … Is anybody here?"

Still nothing.

"Because, you know, if you are here, I'd like to see you. It's okay. You don't have to hide anymore."

More silence. Gregory scanned the room, wondering if he was being watched. He'd heard of some people who worked in Colonial Williamsburg feeling like they were being watched, but he'd never experienced that sensation himself.

And yet, he had been watched, because the woman saw him nearly go into diabetic shock.

"It's okay to show yourself," Gregory called out again. He waited. Nothing.

"Just so you know, I feel like an idiot standing here talking to myself."

Gregory waited in the stillness for another minute. Then he shook his head and laughed, feeling stupider by the moment. This clearly wasn't working.

He walked out of the back of the shop, locking the door behind him. He headed out onto Nicholson Street, debating whether or not he should catch the tour bus back to the Visitor Center where he'd parked. Though it was a nice evening, not too hot and not too cold, he decided he didn't feel like walking all that way. He headed down Colonial Street and then to Duke of Gloucester Street.

The crowd had thinned since the historical buildings closed for the night, but lots of people still milled around. Gregory caught sight of two women dressed in 18th-century clothing walking down the street, likely headed to the bus as well.

Then again, perhaps they were dead.

Gregory should have laughed off the absurd thought, but he couldn't. It wasn't absurd, because he knew how real that ghost woman had seemed. How *alive* she had looked. He didn't recognize the two women, but then he certainly didn't know everybody who worked around here.

The ladies laughed together, and one of them gently punched the other in the shoulder. Okay, so they were alive. Gregory chuckled to himself. He had to get a grip on reality already.

And yet in reality, he had been visited by a ghost. And he wanted to find her. Despite his mental fogginess at the time, Gregory remembered quite clearly what she had looked like in her flower-patterned dress. If he ever saw her again, he would know her right away.

Apart from scanning every woman in the crowd not dressed like a tourist, how would he ever find her again? Did she just haunt the cabinetmaker's shop, or could she wander elsewhere? She knew his name and even about his medical issues, so that clearly hadn't been her first visit with him. How strange. And even a little embarrassing to know she had watched him without his knowledge. He recalled one time he'd changed out of his work clothes and into jeans and a T-shirt when he went to a concert with a friend who was visiting him from Florida.

Had she been watching him then?

The idea didn't bother him as much as it should have. She might be dead, but she was rather attractive.

Good Lord, he really was losing his mind over this. He wasn't ready to give up on finding the ghostly woman, but he wasn't sure how else to go about it. How do you track down a ghost?

The answer stared him squarely in the face. His eyes opened wide as he saw a sign for that evening's ghost tours.

Ghost tours! Why hadn't he thought of that before? Hopefully, they weren't already sold out for the evening.

The ghost tours weren't part of the normal Colonial Williamsburg admission ticket, but they provided something fun for tourists to do after the historical buildings were shut down for the night. Perhaps the tour guide would mention the ghostly woman and he could at least learn more about her.

He turned on his heel and headed to the ghost tour ticket office, located near Bruton Parish Church. He glanced curiously at the graveyard outside the church, suddenly seeing it in a new light, wondering how many of the people buried there still walked the streets of Williamsburg.

After getting a ticket for the 8pm tour, he decided he'd grab dinner at one of the local taverns first, since there wasn't much sense in going home and then coming back for the tour.

Gregory ate dinner at the Christiana Campbell's tavern. He sat at the small bar located downstairs rather than dining alone at a table. It seemed less lonely that way, and he could at least chat with the bartender. He toyed with the idea of asking the bartender if he'd heard any good ghost stories about the area, but ultimately, he decided to wait for the tour.

The tour began promptly in front of the Capitol. Gregory stuck the bright-yellow sticker on his shirt as proof that he had paid for admission and turned his attention to the guide.

"Good evening, folks," greeted the man with a salt-and-pepper beard who reminded Gregory of a skinnier version of Ben. Unlike the daytime Williamsburg tour guides, he wore jeans and a T-shirt instead of colonial dress. "My name is Harry, and I'll be your guide on this ghostly walking tour of Williamsburg. Please be sure to stay with our group, the ones with the yellow stickers, because we do have several other tours going tonight. Also, pay close attention and be very aware of your surroundings."

Harry grinned mischievously and then added, "You never know what unusual things you might experience tonight. It's not unheard of for people on the tour to catch a glimpse of a spirit or even be touched by one! We've heard tales of unseen hands grabbing people's ankles or tapping them on the shoulder, so be on the lookout."

Just a few days ago, Gregory would have thought all that ghost talk was utter nonsense, but now he knew better. Guests had paid for a spooky ghost tour, and clearly this guy was trying to deliver. Though he was sure Harry was likely to embellish some of the tales on this tour, Gregory knew at least some of it was real.

As Harry led the group to the first stop, Gregory pondered what he'd said about ghosts touching things. The woman he'd seen didn't seem to have the ability to touch anything. She didn't even attempt to reach the pills or pick up the bottle. Maybe some spirits were stronger than others.

"So here we have the Capitol building," Harry said, gesturing at the large brick building with circular windows. "First built in 1705, the building was destroyed by fire several times over the years, but now it's been restored."

Gregory already knew the history behind most of the buildings in Williamsburg, but he listened closely anyway in case Harry provided any clues about the woman.

"There have been many reports of supernatural happenings in the Capitol. Doors slamming on empty floors, lights flickering, and even doors suddenly becoming locked ...

from the inside. People have speculated that perhaps even the building itself has a memory, as there was an instance of the fire alarm going off in the middle of the night. Security officers rushed to the scene, only to find the Capitol perfectly intact. There was no rational explanation for the fire alarm going off."

Electrical glitch, Gregory thought, resisting the urge to roll his eyes. He found himself already feeling skeptical, finding it hard to believe stories about unseen hands locking doors. Then he flashed on the memory of the woman pointing out the bottle that Gregory hadn't seen and walking through a solid wooden door.

Gregory shivered a little as they strolled to the next stop, which was the public jail—the gaol as it was labeled with the old spelling of the word.

"The public gaol has had many inhabitants over the years, such as pirates who were accomplices of the infamous Blackbeard, as well as spies, murderers, and military prisoners. There have been lots of strange happenings at the gaol, like coins seemingly falling to the ground out of nowhere, the sounds of ghostly footsteps and, unlike at the Capitol building, doors being mysteriously *unlocked* from the inside."

Gregory seriously doubted that his mystery woman had anything to do with the public gaol, and he was eager for Harry to move on to the next stop. After the group had wandered in and out of the old jail cells, they began walking again. They crossed over a grassy area to get back onto Duke of Gloucester Street.

The group's next stop was the King's Arms Tavern, which was one of the refurbished buildings that now functioned as a working restaurant for lunch and dinner. Harry talked about a woman who haunted the tavern, but it was a more modern-day woman. Her name was Erna, and she'd worked in the tavern and lived above it in an apartment in the 1950s. She'd died suddenly and, according to Harry, her spirit never left. The stories of her teasing and taunting the current waitstaff were interesting, and Gregory couldn't help but find those tales rather believable. After all, the mystery woman had clearly visited him in the cabinetmaker's shop just as Erna was said to still frequent the tavern.

Harry went on to tell the guests that the Alexander Purdie House, which now formed a part of the existing King's Arms Tavern, used to function as a funeral home. Gregory already knew that.

What he didn't know was that several Civil War-era ghosts were said to haunt the King's Arms Tavern. He'd assumed there might be the spirits of Revolutionary soldiers around, but it was easy to forget that Williamsburg saw military action in the 1860s as well.

"The spirit of the funeral home's owner is also said to haunt the building," Harry said. "Guests claim to have felt the icy touch of Delia's cold hands on their bodies."

Gregory felt his eyes go wide, suddenly remembering a cold touch to his face when he had nearly passed out from diabetic shock.

Had the mystery woman touched him?

It would make sense. After all, she had been trying to wake him. Could Delia be the woman he was searching for?

Gregory quickly reasoned it wasn't possible. The funeral home business was founded in the 1800s, and the ghostly woman who had visited him was dressed in typical 1700s clothing.

"There have been fairly frequent sightings of a young woman haunting the Shield's Tavern as well," Harry said.

Gregory drew in a small breath, his hopes rising again.

"Known as the Lady in Green because of her fancy green gown, she has been said to frighten guests and workers by appearing out of thin air."

Dammit.

Gregory's woman wore a lighter, floral dress.

The tour continued much in the same fashion, with Harry telling colorful and interesting ghost stories, but there was no mention of anyone matching the description of Gregory's ghostly savior.

"Our final stop on the tour is one of the most haunted houses in America," Harry said with a grin.

Gregory nodded as they stood in front of the Peyton Randolph House. He had heard rumblings about strange things happening in there. Gregory patiently listened as Harry explained the history of the place, and that Peyton Randolph was one of the founding fathers of this country, though few people today knew who he was. Known as the Father of the Revolution, Randolph requested the First Continental Congress. For all his talk about the desire for freedom, he'd had little to say about freedom for slaves. His family had owned many, and his wife was a particularly nasty slave master.

Harry explained that several of the slaves were said to haunt the place, which was fascinating if unhelpful in answering Gregory's questions. But Gregory knew Peyton Randolph lived from 1721-1775, and the woman's clothing appeared to be from that era. Could she have been one of Randolph's relatives?

"One slave woman is said to haunt the Randolph property, taking a particular interest in Williamsburg guests," Harry said, scanning the small crowd of visitors. "She has a particular dislike for white women, and she's been known to go out of her way to frighten them. Maybe because of her anger toward the cruel Mrs. Randolph."

Gregory wondered if that was true. It was rather sad when you really thought about it. He couldn't blame the slave woman for being angry after the way she'd been treated in life. But how depressing it was to think she was still hanging around the t, the source of her suffering in life, instead of resting in peace.

That also made Gregory wonder about the mystery woman and what was keeping her restless spirit here.

Much to his disappointment, Harry went on to talk about hauntings that had occurred on the property in the 19th century, when the house was owned by the Peachey family. He spoke of two children who were said to haunt the place, as well as Peachey himself, who was buried somewhere on the premises.

"And that concludes our tour for this evening," Harry said with a smile. "I hope you enjoyed yourselves, and I hope you'll remember to always be on the lookout," he said, waggling his eyebrows, "because you never know when a ghost might be around!"

You got that right.

Gregory's shoulders slumped. The tour was over, and he still knew absolutely nothing about the mystery woman. He watched as several of the tourists thanked Harry and gave him a small tip for his services. He fished out his wallet, grabbed a five-dollar bill, and walked over.

When the rest of the tourists had left, he handed the money to Harry.

"Thanks, buddy," he said. "Appreciate it."

"You're welcome," Gregory said. "Hey, can I ask you something?"

"Sure."

"Have you ever actually seen a ghost around here yourself?"

"Oh, there's always a whole lot of strange things happening around here. All the time."

Gregory knew a non-answer when he heard one.

"Listen," Gregory said, lowering his voice. "Just so you know, I'm not just a regular tourist. I work here," he said, gesturing at his work uniform. "Over at Hay's Cabinetmaker's Shop." He laughed softly. "So, you don't have to humor me. I just really want to know."

Harry grinned. "Ah, I hear ya. Well, the answer is no. I haven't actually seen anything with my own eyes, and it annoys me to no end. I'd *love* to have a spiritual encounter, but I haven't yet. That being said, it really does happen all the time around here. Sure, some people make stuff up. Saying something grabbed them or touched them during the tour, but a lot of the experiences are real. I can tell. I know by the way I've seen some people really freak out, you know what I mean?"

Gregory nodded, listening intently.

"So, to answer your question, I've heard a lot of stories over the years, and I'm a believer. I truly am, even though I haven't seen it for myself."

Harry scrutinized him carefully.

"You saw somethin', didn't ya?"

"Yes," Gregory said. "At first, I thought I was imagining things. Hallucinating. I mean, I was pretty sick at the time but ... it was real. I'm sure of that now."

"Wow," Harry said, eyes wide with interest. "Tell me everything."

"It was a woman. Young woman. She had long brown hair and light gray eyes," Gregory said with enthusiasm, grateful to finally have someone to confide in. "She wore a light-colored dress with flowers on it."

"Ahhh, the Weeping Woman," Harry exclaimed.

"You've heard of her? You know who I'm talking about?"

"Yeah, I'm pretty sure I do. As I say, I've never seen her, but I've heard stories about her. People have seen her before, heard her weeping."

Gregory pictured the mystery woman, and the thought of her weeping was awful.

"Do you know who she is? Why she's still here? What happened to her?" Gregory asked, as many more questions formed in his mind.

Harry chuckled, seeming pleased with Gregory's interest. "I don't know much about her. They say she might have been a tavern-keeper's daughter. People think she drowned in the James River."

"Oh," Gregory said somberly. "What else do you know about her?"

"Not much. I just know there are stories about her haunting the streets of Williamsburg and people have heard her weeping." Harry shrugged. "That, and people say they catch the scent of flowers when she's near."

Gregory's eyes grew wide.

"You smelled flowers when you saw her, didn't you?"

"Yeah."

Harry grinned. "Cool. Wish I knew more about her, but that's all I got."

"That helps, though. Thanks a lot."

"Sure thing. You let me know if you see her again, ya hear?" Harry said earnestly.

"You got it. And don't give up. You're bound to see something sooner or later," Gregory assured him.

Harry clapped him on the back. "Thanks, man."

The Weeping Woman. People think she drowned.

Gregory pored over this new information as he headed back to his car.

The woman had drowned. Probably more than two hundred years ago.

But why is she still here?

6

Gregory was looking for me.

Rebekah could hardly believe it. She'd resigned herself to the fact that she would never again be able to watch him adoringly as he worked. And yet, he was searching for her.

She'd been walking aimlessly, invisible, earlier this evening and was surprised to see Gregory in the area after hours. He never stayed late after work unless he was working on a project in the shop. She followed him to see what he was up to.

Buying a ticket for a ghost tour, that's what he was up to. He'd never shown any interest in ghosts before, and she was afraid to hope that she might be the reason he wanted to go on the tour.

Rebekah had followed him into the tavern where he went for dinner, but soon forced herself to leave. Her behavior was stalkerish, even for her, and Gregory deserved better. He was safely around other people in case he'd waited too long to eat again, and that was all that mattered.

However, she simply could not resist joining him on the

ghost tour. She'd heard the tour many times before. After all, they ran nightly. The tales were interesting, some based on truth, others exaggerated or just plain wrong. She hated hearing about herself, and she despised being known as the Weeping Woman. But it was her own damned fault. A few times when she'd been walking around town, fully visible, her mind had wandered to the dark memories of her past. Lost in her pain, sometimes she hardly realized she was crying. Once she came to her senses and realized others were watching, she disappeared so she could wallow in her own misery.

Hence the legend of the Weeping Woman. She supposed it was inevitable that Gregory would hear the story.

She watched Gregory closely during the tour. Although it had only been one day since she'd stopped visiting him at the shop, she already missed him terribly. Her existence was so lonely, and he had been the one bright spot in it. The thought of losing the happiness his mere presence brought was excruciating. What else was left for her to look forward to without him?

Gregory listened intently to every word Harry said, and Rebekah noticed how he perked up at any mention of a ghostly woman. Yes. He was clearly trying to get more information about her. Much to her relief, the subject of the Weeping Woman never came up during this particular tour.

Her relief had been short-lived, however. After Gregory took Harry aside after the tour, Harry had told him about the Weeping Woman. At least he only knew she had drowned. He had no way of knowing the rest of the story.

Gregory looked around for a moment, as if hoping to catch a glimpse of her. It was incredibly tempting to let him know she was right beside him. Sadly, she watched him walk away.

Rebekah wasn't at all sure what to do. Gregory obviously wanted to find her, but why? Curiosity, most likely. She understood. After all, it wasn't every day you saw a ghost. Just a few days ago, she would have given anything for a chance to speak with him. Gregory was a gentleman, and he would never have tried to touch her

If he ever saw her again—if she *allowed* him to see her—he would know he was speaking to a dead woman.

Sure, Gregory *thought* he wanted to see her again, but he might change his mind once it actually happened. Rebekah had seen that scenario play out many times on ghost tours. People thought they wanted a ghostly encounter, but as soon as they got one, they freaked out. When Jackey, one of Peyton Randolph's former slaves, grabbed somebody's ankle, the person usually went nuts.

Rebekah couldn't help chuckling when she recalled the time she saw Jackey do that to a nasty woman who had uttered a racial slur. Hopefully, the wretched lady had gotten scared enough to never say such a horrible thing again.

She watched Gregory until he disappeared into the distance. She still had no idea what to do.

Should she try to approach him, or should she simply let him go?

7

Gregory headed out the back door of the shop promptly at closing time, locking the door behind him. He turned, took one step forward, and then he gasped.

There, standing a few feet away on the bridge over the small stream, was the mystery woman.

The Weeping Woman.

He froze, too scared to move.

She smiled and said softly, "I hear you've been looking for me."

Still unable to speak, he nodded. She was just as he'd remembered her. Long brown hair, gentle gray eyes, and she wore the same floral dress. Of course she did. What was she going to do, change into jeans and a T-shirt? The thought was so absurd, he nearly laughed. But he didn't. Every muscle in his body was tense.

"It's okay," the woman said gently. "It's safe to come closer. I can't hurt you. I can't even touch you, see?"

With that, she moved her hand *through the railing of the wooden bridge.*

Gregory let out a quiet, strangled noise. Her motion hadn't been threatening, but it was utterly surreal. Otherworldly.

"Sorry," she said, wincing. "I guess I'm trying to get you used to the idea of being around a ghost."

He drew in a deep breath to steady himself, then let it out slowly. He'd been trying so hard to find the mystery woman, he hadn't considered what to do once he did. His rational brain grappled with the notion that he was looking at someone who had died, and yet she was still speaking.

She stood there, patiently waiting for him to come to her.

She looked rather somber. Gathering his nerve, he walked forward and stopped near her, but not too close, on the bridge.

She waited a moment, then she asked quietly, "Are you afraid of me?"

The woman's expression was tender, and she seemed so concerned at the thought of scaring him that his fear began to ease. Gregory stared at her for a few seconds. "You saved my life."

"You didn't answer my question."

He chuckled. "A little."

"There's nothing to fear with me," she said, her voice sounding tired and somewhat defensive. "I may be a ghost, but I'm still a woman."

Gregory looked into her eyes, feeling pained by the weariness on her face. "You're a *beautiful* woman."

Her expression softened, and she gazed at him with gratitude, as if she'd been dying of thirst and he'd handed her a glass of ice-cold water. After several seconds, she said in a voice that was nearly a whisper, "Thank you."

Gregory wondered if she was used to having people

scream and run at the sight of her. She seemed grateful for this simple human contact.

"You must have so many questions," she said.

"One very important one."

She nodded, encouraging him to ask.

"What's your name?"

Her face broke into a lovely smile. She had probably expected him to ask her questions about life after death or how she died. Naturally, he was burning to ask those things, but he felt it was more important to treat her with respect and kindness. He wouldn't ask a living person he'd just met any personal questions.

"Rebekah," she answered. "Spelled the old-timey way. R-e-b-e-k-a-h."

Gregory chuckled. "Old-timey. I like that. Rebekah is a beautiful name. It suits you."

She graced him with another lovely smile. He marveled at how easy it was to make her happy. After what she'd done for him, he was glad for any opportunity to even begin to repay her.

"And you ... somehow ... already know my name," he said.

"Yes, Gregory. I already knew your name because ..." She laughed nervously. "It's hard to explain without sounding like a crazy person. The truth is I like to watch you work. I can be invisible when I want to be. And in my situation I can get pretty bored, as you might imagine. I can't travel too far away from this area. I'm rather stuck, so I like to watch Williamsburg employees, like you. I think I've gotten everyone's tour guide speeches memorized. I was there the day you started work at Hay's Cabinetmaker's Shop, when you talked to Ben and told him about your medical history. You told him where you would keep your tablets in case of an emergency."

"Ah, I see," Gregory said. "Well, I'm grateful for that."

"Me too," Rebekah said, her gray eyes filled with worry. She watched him for a moment then shyly lowered her gaze. "So, it's not only you that I watch during the day. But y—y—you're ... well, you're my favorite."

"Really? Why?"

Rebekah looked away for a moment, and then lifted her gaze again so she could meet his eye. "You're quite handsome for one thing."

He laughed, feeling his face get slightly hot. It was strange. Here he was blushing while he flirted with a *ghost*. He'd actually forgotten for a moment that Rebekah was dead.

Dead.

He still couldn't quite wrap his head around it.

"And I like the way you talk to the children," Rebekah continued. "You're good with them. You don't condescend to them. I also like to watch you craft such beautiful furniture. Best of all, I love to hear you play the harpsichord."

Gregory grinned. "I love music."

"I know," she said. The softness in her voice and the tenderness in her expression told him that she did know. He suspected Rebekah already understood his passion for music much more than his ex-wife ever did.

"Do you like music?" he asked.

"Very much. I used to sing a lot. I don't anymore." Rebekah looked down at the ground again.

Gregory wanted to ask why, but he got the impression she didn't want to talk about it.

She shook her head as if to ward off whatever negative thought she might be having, and then she brightened.

"You're my favorite to watch, but there are others. I mean, who doesn't enjoy watching Orlando?"

"Yes!" Gregory agreed with a laugh. "He is quite a character."

Orlando Blake was literally *in* character when he walked the streets of Colonial Williamsburg. While Gregory merely dressed in 18th-century clothing, Orlando played various fictional characters and real historical figures as part of his job. A wannabe actor, he was indeed highly entertaining to both guests and employees of the historical district. Though Gregory didn't know him all that well, he did find him easy to talk to. They'd sat together in the shade on a warm day once during their lunch break, and Gregory had somehow found himself confiding in Orlando about his divorce. It had felt good to get some things off his chest.

"Orlando's handsome, too, don't you think?" he teased, making Rebekah laugh.

"Oh, yes. I can't argue with that. He even manages to make those ridiculous powdered wigs look good."

"So that's what you do all day? People watch?"

"Pretty much. What else have I to do?" Rebekah said, holding out her ghostly hands. "Gregory, I do want you to know I never violated your privacy. Or at least, I hope I didn't. I'm sure it must be strange to think I was around and you didn't know it."

Gregory nodded. Yes, it certainly was an odd feeling.

"I was only with you when there were other people around. I mean, for the most part, anyway. I usually leave when you lock up for the night, or even when there aren't any tourists around. People act differently when they think they're alone, so I try not to watch people in their private time. I confess I did hang around that night when you were finishing up the card table leg." Rebekah dropped her eyes again. "You were just doing such beautiful work ..."

"It's okay. I don't mind. Especially since, well, I don't know what might have happened if you weren't there."

Rebekah physically shuddered at the thought. Her movements were so *real*. It must be easy for her to pass as a living, breathing person.

"Most of the time, I guess it doesn't matter if you watch what I'm doing at work. It must be boring, though." Gregory said, shaking his head.

"Not at all," she reassured him.

"There was that time I changed my clothes at work."

"I remember that," Rebekah exclaimed, eyes wide. "My God, Gregory, you barely gave me a chance to escape in time. You must have been in quite a hurry. No sooner did you shut and lock the door did you whip your shirt right off!"

He laughed as he remembered doing just that. He hadn't wanted to be late for the concert, and he'd needed to hightail it out of there. "So, did you like what you saw?"

Rebekah hung her head, and Gregory was afraid he had embarrassed her. Then she lifted her head and gazed admiringly at him and he couldn't help being flattered.

He surveyed her curiously, wanting to ask so many things, but not wanting to upset her. She seemed so grateful to have a normal conversation with him, he hated to bring up the subject of death.

"It's okay to ask me questions," Rebekah said after he'd been quiet for a bit.

"Are you the one they call the Weeping Woman?"

She appeared to let out a sigh, but there was no breath involved in the motion.

"Yes. I'm not crazy about that name, but yes. I suppose that's me."

"Why do you weep?" Gregory asked. He hated to think of her crying.

After a long pause, she said, "Regret. Also, loneliness."

"Are there others like you? Other spirits? I guess they must be everywhere around here, huh?"

"There are some. Not as many as there used to be. I've made friends with other ghosts in the past, but I don't anymore. Because they always go away," she said with a sad smile. "I've been around a long, long time, and I've seen a lot of people come and go. Most people aren't stuck on Earth when they die. They usually go where they're supposed to go."

"You mean Heaven?" Gregory asked, utterly fascinated.

"Yes."

"Wow!"

His enthusiasm made Rebekah laugh. It felt good to see her face light up after having looked sorrowful just moments ago.

"Even most of the spirits stuck here eventually cross over to Heaven. For me, it's like getting older even though my physical form never changes. It's like living to be a hundred years old or something. You get to that age, and pretty much everyone you loved is gone."

"No wonder you're so lonely," Gregory said, feeling a sharp stab of empathy in his chest. It made sense that Rebekah would spend her days watching him and Orlando and the other workers here. My God, she must be desperate for any human contact. And yet, she seemed to prefer to remain invisible most of the time.

"You could probably talk to people on the street, right? And they'd never know. Do you ever do that?"

"Sometimes," she said. "It's hard, though."

"Why?"

"Mainly because it's so risky. I can get away with talking to people if I don't get too close. But if they try to touch me ..."

Rebekah winced as she spoke.

"That's happened before, hasn't it?"

"Yes. Once I was talking to a young couple late in the evening. They saw the way I'm dressed, and of course they thought I worked here. They asked me for directions to the King's Arms Tavern. I'm always happy to help people like that. I know everything there is to know about this place, and I enjoy answering questions from tourists."

"Me too."

She gazed into his eyes. "I know. It shows in the way you speak to them. Anyway, I chatted with them for a few minutes, and it was easy to forget my ... situation. For a few minutes, it felt like I was a normal tour guide, just helping them out. Well, the young woman had hurt her foot somehow, and she was on crutches. When she and her husband turned to go, she stumbled into me."

"And she fell *through* you," Gregory said gently.

"I'll never forget the sound of their screams. Thank God there weren't too many people around, and there weren't any children nearby."

Her expression was so pained that he could hardly bear it. "I can't stand having people be afraid of me. I don't want to be a monster, Gregory."

Her voiced hitched as if she were crying, but no actual tears came.

"You're not a monster, Rebekah," Gregory assured her.

"Thank you. Thank you for treating me like a person

and not a ghoul. Oh, I hated that you were afraid of me," she said sorrowfully.

"I was afraid. But I'm not anymore."

"Good."

"It was quite a shock at first. You know, to see you appear and disappear and all that. But now? Standing here talking to you, it's easy to forget that you're ..."

"Dearly departed?" she said with a laugh.

Gregory laughed too. "Exactly."

"It helps me forget, too, for a while. It's wonderful having a conversation with a handsome man and not be afraid you'll discover my secret, since you already know." After a brief pause, she spoke again. "Can I ask you a question?"

"Of course."

"Do I really smell like flowers?"

He grinned. "Yes. The scent of lilacs."

"Oh, I've always loved flowers. They put lots of lilacs on my—" She stopped short as if not wanting to ruin the moment.

"Grave," Gregory finished for her.

"Yes."

"Do you mind if I ask ... what happened?" Gregory ventured carefully. "You were obviously pretty young when you passed."

"I drowned," she said matter-of-factly. "In 1762. I was twenty years old." Her face hardened. "What else do you want to know?" Rebekah asked, her expression softening again as she spoke. "If I were you, I would want to know what it's like to be a ghost."

"Yes. I'm definitely curious about that."

"Well, as you can tell, I can see and hear, but I can't touch anything. I can't smell or taste, either."

"Do you miss eating food?"

"Not really. I guess I miss the idea of it sometimes. I used to really enjoy tea and sweet things, like cakes and such. I miss the social part of food, too. Sitting down to a meal with family and friends, that sort of thing. But I'm never hungry, and I can't smell the food, so it's not like it really bothers me much that I can't eat."

"If you could have any food in the world right now, what would it be?" he asked.

Rebekah laughed and seemed delighted at the question. "My goodness. That's easy. Gingerbread. I love gingerbread. The smell, the taste, the texture. Definitely my favorite."

"So, gingerbread with a nice cup of tea."

"Yes!" she said, her eyes alight with happiness. "Yes, that would be perfect."

"Rebekah, I wish more than anything that I could take you over to the Raleigh Tavern right now and get you some fresh gingerbread and tea."

"Thank you, Gregory. That's so sweet of you to say."

"I mean it. If you were, you know, *available*, I'd ask you out on a date in a hot minute," Gregory told her.

Rebekah stared at him. He began to worry that he had upset her. She remained quiet for an uncomfortably long time.

"Umm, you okay?"

She laughed, snapping out of whatever trance she'd been in.

"Yes, yes I'm fine. It's just ... that means a lot to me. It's been quite some time since anyone's treated me like a woman. And it's been a long time since I felt like one, if that makes any sense. I think you're a wonderful man, Gregory Markham, and I couldn't be more honored that you would actually want to take me out on a date. It means more than you know."

Gregory smiled, his heart breaking for her. He couldn't begin to understand what it must be like to exist the way she did. No friends, no family. Utterly alone. Everyone she cared about had gone away.

Well she wasn't alone anymore. She had him for a friend now.

"Do you know why you're still here? Why you haven't gone to Heaven yet?" Gregory ventured carefully.

"Yes," Rebekah said sadly. He waited for her to continue. Avoiding his gaze, she added, "I don't deserve to go to Heaven."

"That can't be true," Gregory said firmly. Kindness radiated from this woman, not to mention that she had saved his life.

Rebekah looked down, her face suddenly filled with a depth of sorrow that he had never seen before. As much as Gregory wanted to know what had happened, he resisted asking.

"So, I guess you must have lived in this area, too?" he asked, changing the subject with as much grace as he could muster. "Do you go visit where you used to live?"

"I do," she said. "My father owned Jennings Tavern, and we lived above it. My mother and my father, my older sister, Martha, and my younger brother, Nathaniel."

"Oh wow, that's so cool," Gregory exclaimed. Jennings Tavern was located on Duke of Gloucester Street, not too far from the cabinetmaker's shop. Like the Peyton Randolph House, it was one of the original restored buildings in the area. A major archaeological dig had been done in the 1960s, and they'd found lots of artifacts that had helped them reconstruct the building.

Rebekah laughed, amused at his excitement.

"It's a gorgeous building," Gregory said. In addition to

the main tavern, there were several small buildings outside. The outbuildings existed to keep the slaves away from the genteel guests of the taverns.

Gregory knew Mr. Jennings had owned at least a dozen slaves.

He wanted to ask Rebekah how she felt about that—how she'd felt at the time about owning slaves, and what her feelings were now. Curious as he was, he didn't want to sound judgmental or make her feel uncomfortable.

"Gregory, you need to go!" she said suddenly.

"What? Why?" he asked, snapping back to the present.

"It's getting late," she said, her voice filled with concern. "You haven't eaten yet."

"Oh, I'll be okay. I had a snack earlier."

"Even so. You need to go get some dinner." Her pretty face was full of worry

A pleasant tingling sensation rippled through Gregory's body having a beautiful woman make a fuss over him. It might be ridiculous since she was dead, but somehow that didn't matter. "Okay, I will." He paused. Now it was his turn to worry. "I feel bad leaving you alone. Where do you go at night? When there's nobody around?"

"Well, if I choose, I can just vanish for a while. Vanishing is like being invisible, but it's more than that. I can disappear for as long as I like, and I'm not conscious. It's God's way of giving spirits a break from this existence perhaps."

Rebekah smiled wearily.

"That's good, I guess. So you don't have to be wandering alone all night at least."

"Right. And that's why when people spend the night in a haunted place, not everyone will have a ghostly encounter. It could be the ghosts temporarily vanished. Also, there are people who are more naturally sensitive to the presence of spirits," Rebekah said, then giggled.

"What's so funny?"

"You're not one of those sensitive people, Gregory," Rebekah said with fondness in her voice. He rather enjoyed the affectionate way she said his name. "There are people that can feel my presence when I'm near. They look up, feeling like there's someone around. You never knew when I was there."

"Interesting."

"Yes. So, when people are hoping to see or feel a ghost in a haunted house and they don't, it could be because they're not naturally attuned to the spiritual, or it could be due to ghosts vanishing. Just because a house is haunted doesn't mean there are ghosts around all the time."

"This is all so fascinating. I could stand here and talk to you all night, Rebekah."

"As much as I love hearing you say that, I will not allow it. Go eat your dinner!"

"Yes, ma'am," he said in a teasing voice. "I would really love to talk with you again."

"Well, that most certainly can be arranged. We'll talk again soon, Gregory. I promise."

"Good."

It was difficult to leave Rebekah for the night, but he knew he had to go.

"Adieu!" Gregory said. "'I have too grieved a heart to take a tedious leave.'"

Rebekah's eyes flew open wide and she nearly shouted, "*The Merchant of Venice!*"

"Yes!" he said with astonishment that Rebekah had recognized the relatively obscure quote from Shakespeare. He could have gone with the old "parting is such sweet sorrow" from *Romeo and Juliet*, but he was glad he'd chosen a different line.

"Oh, I just *adore* Shakespeare," Rebekah said happily.

"Me too. I minored in English in college and took a class on Shakespeare."

"Me too! I mean, not about the minor, but I've taken many classes on Shakespeare in college."

"Really?" Gregory asked, confused. "I thought, you know, back in your day, they weren't too keen on women and book-learnin'."

Rebekah laughed. "Oh, yes. You're quite right about that. There's no way I could have attended college back when I was alive, but I was taught to read and write. And I suppose I should say I audited the Shakespeare classes rather than taking them. Over at the College of William and Mary. They usually have a Shakespeare class in either the fall or the spring, and I sit in every time."

Gregory grinned. "That's brilliant."

"I don't have the ability to travel too far from this area, and I was so happy when I discovered there were classes I could reach within the boundaries I can wander.

"Oh, I was so happy when I discovered that class. I sit in on others, too, but Shakespeare is my favorite. I used to read him all the time when I was alive. I especially adore the sonnets and the love stories."

He found Rebekah's dreamy voice quite endearing. She loved flowers, music, and love stories. Her girly-girl nature was sweet, and Gregory found it easy to get swept up in her enthusiasm.

"Okay, go now. I mean it!"

"I'm going, I'm going. You don't have to be invisible when you come visit, okay? Just come in and see me."

"I will, Gregory. I promise. 'Good night, good night.

Parting is such sweet sorrow. That I shall say good night 'til it be morrow.'"

As if to ensure he left for the night, she faded away until he could no longer see her.

From anyone else, that *Romeo and Juliet* quote would have sounded cheesy. But not from Rebekah's lips. From her, it sounded sweet and sensuous.

My God, he thought, *I'm smitten with a ghost.*

8

Rebekah was deliriously happy at having been able to speak to Gregory, to see him smile at her instead of shrinking back in terror.

Beautiful. He had called her *beautiful. He would have asked her out if she were alive.*

Rebekah could hardly believe it. She knew she was getting carried away. After all, what did it matter if he *would* have asked her out? It wasn't possible. Besides, for all she knew, Gregory was simply being kind because that was the type of person he was. Dear and gentle and kind.

Well, that was more than enough for Rebekah.

It had been more than two hundred years since a gentleman had paid her any real attention. For the first time in an achingly long time, Rebekah didn't feel lonely. She wouldn't even vanish tonight. No. She wanted to stay conscious and fully immerse herself in the euphoria she felt after being in Gregory's presence.

Though she relished the chance to revel in her romantic fantasies of Gregory Markham, she found herself wishing she had someone to share her feelings with. A girlfriend.

Better yet, her older sister, Martha. In life, Rebekah had been envious when her sister met and married a wonderfully handsome man named Philip. Oh, he was so dashing. Despite her jealousy, Rebekah had been happy for her sister to have found love. Philip was a terrific husband and went on to become a warm and loving father to their children. Rebekah had always dreamed of meeting a man like Philip, and then marrying him and bearing his children.

Of course, that had never happened. In all the time she had existed, in life and in this afterlife she'd endured, she had never met that man of her dreams.

Until now.

Rebekah shook her head, laughing somberly. It was indeed like something out of a Shakespearean tragedy. She knew Gregory didn't feel the same way about her. Rebekah was passionately in love with him, while he had merely flirted with her. If she disappeared tomorrow, he would likely forget all about her.

Rebekah shook off that depressing thought. Though she knew there could not possibly be any future for them, and he would never love her the way she did him, she would not dwell on that now. Instead, she would indulge in all her silly romantic notions about Gregory. Privately, she would cling to them, for they were all she had.

"Hear my soul speak. Of the very instant that I saw you, did my heart fly at your service."

That line from Shakespeare's *The Tempest* truly said it best. It had felt like she'd loved Gregory at first sight. And, though she would never be able to love him with her body, she truly loved him from her soul. Rebekah's heart and soul were all she had left, and they were his for the taking.

Rebekah walked the darkened streets of Williamsburg, invisible, lost in her fantasies. She would visit him at the shop as he'd invited her to, but not first thing in the morning. She would force herself to wait until the afternoon, so as not to appear too eager. It was silly, she knew. It wasn't like she had any pressing engagements now, or for the rest of her existence, and Gregory knew it. Even so, she would wait just a bit. She might be dead, but she still had her pride.

Drifting aimlessly, Rebekah daydreamed about Gregory tenderly kissing her and holding her in his arms. She even imagined him making love to her, both gently and urgently at the same time. In life, she had always hoped to meet the man of her dreams and fall in love, just like all those love stories and Shakespearean sonnets. She had longed to know what it was like to experience physical love with a man, but she'd never gotten the chance.

Always a hopeless romantic, at times like this, Rebekah was grateful for her vivid imagination. She didn't care if she was being ridiculous, since this situation could only end in heartbreak. She was determined to live, or simply *exist*, in the moment. She was more in love with Gregory Markham than ever before, and she was determined to enjoy this feeling while it lasted.

9

Gregory waited impatiently all morning for Rebekah to show up. He tried to convince himself it was the curiosity of befriending a ghost, but he was kidding himself. He wanted to see *her*. He couldn't remember the last time he'd had such a fascinating conversation with a woman. Some of what made it so fascinating was learning about death and the afterlife, of course, but it was more than that. Rebekah was easy to talk to, and he had been very much at ease with her. Incredible, considering how terrified he'd been of her at first. How quickly that had all changed.

It was humanly impossible for there to be anything physical between them, yet it *was* physical. Gregory's heartbeat sped up and his body tingled all over like some schoolboy with a crush whenever he thought of her.

All morning long, Gregory had eagerly looked around, hoping to see her. He briefly considered the possibility she could be there already and was invisible to him. She wouldn't do that anymore, though. He was fairly certain she would respect his wishes.

It wasn't until after lunch that Rebekah finally showed up. The door to the shop opened and, at first, Gregory was disappointed to see an older couple enter. He grinned widely as Rebekah slipped in just behind them. She met his gaze and smiled back.

The older couple explored the shop for a few minutes, admiring the fancy woodworking items on display. Then they politely greeted Gregory and left shortly after.

"I've been waiting all day for you," he said, not bothering to hide his eagerness because he knew it would make her smile. It did.

"I've been outside for a little while now. I had to wait for some people to come to visit and open the door."

"You could have just come in through the wall any time you wanted," Gregory said.

"What if there had been other people in here already?" Rebekah asked. "I would have frightened them to death."

"You could have floated in while you were invisible to check, and then just turned visible once you saw the coast was clear."

"Yes," Rebekah responded. "I suppose I could have."

"Anything to get you in here faster."

Her eyes lit up with pleasure, and Gregory felt warm all over. He couldn't imagine the crushing loneliness she had endured in her state, and he wanted to do everything he could to make her feel cherished.

"How has your day been so far?" she asked, glancing around the shop.

"Good. Busy enough to keep me from being bored, but not overcrowded."

"You're almost done the card table," Rebekah said, gazing admiringly at his work.

"Yep. I'm pretty happy with the way it's turning out,"

Gregory said, inspecting one of the legs of the table on his work bench.

"It's beautiful," she said. Gregory watched her eyes as she gazed at the table.

"Thanks. You can come back here with me if you want to," he said, gesturing to the rope that separated his workspace from the general public. "Dressed like that, people will assume you work here anyway. Except for the fact that you don't wear a bonnet."

Her face fell for an instant, and it occurred to him that her lack of headwear could be due to her drowning death.

"It's okay. Nobody's around," he said, eager to distract her in case her thoughts had drifted to her demise.

She grimaced slightly and walked through the rope so she could stand next to him.

"It doesn't creep me out anymore, you know," he said.

"I'm grateful for that," Rebekah said. He could see the look of relief on her face. "I just want to appear as *normal* as much as possible."

"I understand."

He wondered again what was keeping her trapped here and if there was anything he could do to help. Maybe once she got to know him better, she might trust him enough to confide in him.

Rebekah scanned the woodworking room. Slabs of wood leaned against the walls while various metal tools with wooden handles hung above them. Ornately carved chair backs and arms hung on pegs and wood shavings littered the floor. "They really did an incredible job of restoring this place. It looks a lot like it did back in the day."

"Oh, wow. You must have actually been in here back in the 1700s."

Rebekah nodded. "I remember coming in here with my

father. It's really amazing what the Colonial Williamsburg Foundation has done with the place. These drafting tables were right here, just as you have them."

She gestured to the two long wooden tables where Gregory and Ben did most of their carpentry work.

"And all these tools on the walls. Of course, that grandfather clock was about six inches to the left of where it is now."

"Wow," Gregory said.

Rebekah giggled. "I'm joking with you. I don't remember *that* much. I was a child when I came here, and it was more than two hundred and fifty years ago."

Gregory chuckled. "Fair enough."

"It really does look much like I remember, though."

After all the time he'd spent working in here and thinking about the past and the people who had been on this very spot over two centuries ago, it was surreal to speak to one of those people. He could only imagine how excited the local historians would be if they had any idea there were ghosts from the 18th century around who could provide invaluable insight into the past.

"I love to watch you work, Gregory," Rebekah said, studying his hands as they etched fine details into the table leg. "Your hands are so big, and yet you can still do such detailed work."

Gregory flushed, pleased with Rebekah's compliment. He rather liked that she'd noticed the size of his hands. He found himself imagining all the things he could do with those hands, if only he could touch her.

Just as Gregory was thinking how nice it was to be alone with Rebekah, the back door to the shop swung open and he heard several footsteps. Voices indicated several children were present. Normally, he would have been pleased to see a bunch of kids coming to visit, but he found himself slightly annoyed at the interruption.

Reminding himself that he was at work and it was his job to help ensure these nice folks had an enjoyable vacation, Gregory got up from his worktable and walked out into the hallway. He called out to them. "Good afternoon. Welcome."

"Thank you," the mother said politely.

Gregory went back to his worktable, knowing he'd get another chance to be alone with Rebekah soon. She had plenty of time on her hands.

The three boys, ranging in age from about six to thirteen, peered at the wood crafts.

"Don't touch," the mother gently reminded the youngest boy.

"Oh cool. A coffin!" said the oldest.

Rebekah laughed and exchanged a knowing glance with Gregory. It was fun. Like they had an inside joke to share.

If you think that coffin is cool, come check out the lady who's been in one.

The tourists wandered into the shop room where Gregory was sitting.

"Oh, that looks nice," the mom said. "What is that you're working on?"

"A card table. It's made of mahogany," Gregory said, lifting up one of the legs to show off his handiwork.

"Oh, that's beautiful," she said.

"Thanks. Take your time, look around, and let me know if you have any questions."

On second thought, Gregory was glad that this nice family had come to visit. It felt good to have Rebekah see him at work. He wished someone would ask him a history question so he could show off his historical knowledge.

The door suddenly flung open with such force that everyone jumped. Only one person Gregory knew could make an entrance like that.

Orlando Blake.

Orlando often gave boisterous speeches in front of the Capitol or the courthouse, and people would gather around to watch. Other times, he would wander into some of the buildings to start discussions and stir up fake trouble. Gregory usually enjoyed visits from Orlando. He certainly knew how to liven things up, and the tourists had lots of fun with him.

"Hello, fellow colonials!" Orlando boomed in his loud stage voice. "Good day to you!"

The parents and three boys all looked up in amusement at Orlando. He wore a tricorn hat and a tan-colored wool, button-down coat. To Gregory's annoyance, he realized Rebekah was right when she'd said Orlando managed to make even those silly powdered wigs look good, with his classical masculine good looks, chiseled jaw, and sensual brown eyes.

Rebekah's eyes lit up at the sight of him, and a sudden, unbidden surge of jealously tore through Gregory. It took him by surprise. He'd never been the jealous type, even though his ex-wife was quite popular and had flirted with everybody. He wanted Rebekah all to himself today.

Orlando strode confidently up to the family of five, standing a few feet away from Gregory's worktable. Gregory watched him as he sized up his audience. He had to admit he'd always admired the way Orlando never grabbed a random "volunteer" from his audience to take part in his shenanigans. He only chose people who were cool with it, and he was gentler with shyer tourists. He didn't ignore the quiet ones, but he took care not to embarrass them. If they laughed and played along, he'd keep up his antics. If not, he'd dial it back so as not to put them on the spot.

"And what colony are you fine folks from?" Orlando inquired.

"Tell him what state you're from," the father said quietly to his oldest son, the one in his early teens.

"Oh. Minnesota," the boy said with a grin.

"Minnnnn-e-sooo-ta," Orlando said, scratching his chin and looking confused. "I don't think I'm familiar with that."

"It's one of the new colonies," the mother said, her eyes dancing with amusement. "Up north."

"You don't say!" Orlando shook his head. "I am confounded. I am *confounded*."

The two older boys and their parents chuckled, while the six-year-old looked a little confused.

"Well, hello there, my fine fellow," Orlando said, directing his attention to the little boy, his friendly brown eyes scanning for any signs of discomfort.

"Hi!" the little guy chirped happily.

Orlando grinned at the kid. "You look like a fine, strapping young man. You'd make a good soldier." He bent down and cupped a hand near his mouth, muttering conspiratorially, "You're not loyal to the king, are ya?"

The boy eyed Orlando, not quite sure what to make of him.

"Say no, Brian," the father said with a laugh.

"No!" Brian replied with confidence.

"Splendid!" Orlando said, straightening up. Little Brian giggled, likely pleased that he'd gotten the answer right.

The parents and kids went back to looking at the wooden crafts in the hallway.

Orlando turned to Rebekah, standing next to Gregory.

She kept her distance from Orlando, safe behind the velvet rope where he wouldn't come near enough to touch her.

"Well, hello, Miss," Orlando said with a bow.

"Hello, good sir," she responded with a coy smile.

He eyed Rebekah with interest, clearly finding her attractive. Gregory's chest tightened. That guy was a force of nature. He had a way of commanding attention anywhere he went, and Gregory felt boring by comparison. Orlando breezed in and made everyone laugh, while Gregory quietly went about his woodworking.

"And what occasion might bring a lovely young woman such as yourself to the cabinetmaker's shop?" Orlando asked Rebekah flirtatiously.

"I'm here to enquire on the progress of a card table that was commissioned for my father, the owner of Jennings Tavern," she responded with a twinkle in her eye.

"Oh, I see," he said, his eyes lingering on her.

Gregory gripped the card table so hard, he might have broken it had he not released his grasp in time. He glanced up at Orlando, whose eyes opened wide. He held up his hands in mock defense and took an exaggerated step back.

Clearly, Gregory had done a poor job of disguising his jealousy and possessiveness.

Rebekah stifled a giggle, and he felt his face get hot. What was it about this woman that brought out such strong emotions in him?

"I best take my leave," Orlando said, looking amused. As much as it annoyed Gregory, he knew Orlando was right to be entertained at his antics. Gregory was acting like an idiot.

"See ya around," Gregory said, doing his best to sound light and cheerful as Orlando strutted out the door.

The tourist family also headed out.

"Thank you!" the mother called with a friendly wave at Gregory.

"You're welcome. Have a good day now," he said.

He was pleased when Rebekah went back to admiring his table as he went back to work. He tried to put Orlando's dashing good looks and charming personality out of his head, but it was tough.

"I bet Orlando isn't even his real name," Gregory muttered. It was such an actor name. A little too perfect.

"It isn't," Rebekah said.

Gregory eyed her curiously, and she shrugged.

"I hear things."

"What's his real name? Do you know?"

"Yes," she said. "But I can't tell you."

"Why can't you tell me?"

"Well," she said thoughtfully. "I mean, I could tell you, but it's kind of personal to him. He doesn't like his real name, and there's a reason he goes by Orlando. You should just ask him sometime. He'll probably tell you. It's not like he told me. I overheard him talking about it, so I wouldn't feel right telling you. Just ask him."

"Does the name have anything to do with Shakespeare's character Orlando?"

Rebekah hesitated for a moment. "Yes. But that's all I'm going to say."

He resisted the urge to grumble out loud about this guy who was actually a nice person and even sort of a friend. He was unsettled by how out-of-sorts he felt.

"Gregory?" Rebekah asked in a soft voice.

"Yeah?"

"Would you do something for me?"

He gazed into her pretty gray eyes. "Of course. Anything."

"Would you play the harpsichord?"

Honored by her request, Gregory immediately set down his tools. "I'd love to."

He wiped his hands on a nearby rag and headed over to the harpsichord against the wall. Rebekah followed. He watched her eyes as she surveyed the large wooden instrument that was somewhat similar to a piano.

"I can't believe you made this," she said.

"Well, I didn't make it all by myself. Ben helped a lot."

"It's lovely. Just *lovely.*"

The harpsichord wasn't as intricately designed as the card table and some of the other items Gregory had crafted, but it had turned out nicely. It was made of dark, solid wood with a fine finish. He was quite proud of it, and he enjoyed the impressive looks from tourists when he informed them that he'd helped make it.

"Thanks," Gregory said with a grin. He sat down at the harpsichord and thought about several songs he could play from memory without digging out the sheet music. He chose a sonata with a pretty melody.

Gregory played the piece with passion and flourish, partially because he was acutely aware of Rebekah's presence. He loved music, and it was easy for him to get lost in the beauty and pleasure of it as his fingers danced across the keys, even when he was alone. He felt incredibly lucky that playing the harpsichord to entertain guests was part of his job.

After finishing the song, Gregory glanced up, eager to see Rebekah's reaction. He was not disappointed. She looked enraptured.

"That was beautiful." She placed a hand near her heart as though she was able to touch her own chest. "Just beautiful. Will you play another?"

It was such a simple request, and yet it meant so much to him. More than Rebekah could possibly understand.

"Be happy to." He launched into another song. The back door of the shop opened, and he heard several people enter. Upon hearing the music, the tourists entered quietly and respectfully, heading straight to the back of the shop where Gregory was playing.

Out of the corner of his eye, he saw Rebekah glance up and smile at the tourists and then go back to watching him play.

His feelings of jealousy and inadequacy began to fade away. Sure, Orlando was outgoing, funny, and handsome, but Rebekah seemed the romantic type. She loved pretty things, like Shakespeare's love stories and flowers. And music and artistic woodworking crafts. Many of the things he liked as well. Things he was good with.

Gregory couldn't hide his smile.

10

Gregory was pleased when Rebekah came into the shop in the morning the next day. There was just one problem.

Ben was working. Without him here, Gregory could pass Rebekah off as just another employee at the shop, and tourists were none the wiser. Standing safely behind the velvet rope, people assumed she and Gregory worked together in Hay's Cabinetmaker's Shop. Ben, however, would know Rebekah wasn't on the payroll.

"Good morning," Rebekah said, walking in the door behind an older couple. While the man and woman lingered in the hallway, Rebekah came straight to the back of the shop. She glanced at Ben and exchanged a knowing look with Gregory. She couldn't stay today, and they both knew it.

"Good morning!" Ben said in a friendly voice.

"Ben, this is Rebekah J—" Gregory stopped before he said Rebekah Jennings, which would inevitably result in Ben asking if she was related to the past owners of the

Jennings Tavern down the road. "Rebekah. She's a friend of mine."

"Oh, well very nice to meet you," Ben said.

Gregory was a little worried that Ben might ask questions about where she worked, but thankfully he didn't.

"Very nice to meet you too," Rebekah said, eying the back door nervously. She didn't want to stay too long, just in case, but it wasn't like she could open the door and walk out.

"Hey, I wanted to ask you something while you're here," Gregory said, jumping up from his seat at the carpentry table. He headed to the back door and opened it for her. "This will just take a sec," he said to Ben, who nodded.

Gregory led Rebekah out the door and shut it safely behind him. They walked over the small bridge where they had first spoken.

"Sorry about that," he said, nodding toward the shop. "I didn't even think about him being here today."

"It's okay," Rebekah said, sounding disappointed. "I should have remembered he usually works on Saturdays." Ben's presence probably meant she would be forced to spend the day alone, which saddened Gregory immensely.

"Hey, do you want to meet me for lunch? I mean, do you want to meet and watch me eat *my* lunch?" he asked with a laugh.

"Of course. I would love it."

"Okay, cool. I'll meet ya out on Duke of Gloucester Street across from Market Square at about noon?"

"Sure. I'll try to fit you into my busy schedule," Rebekah said with a smile.

∽

Rebekah sat beneath Gregory's usual tree on Duke of Gloucester Street, waiting for him. Scanning the people strolling down the street, her phantom heart leapt in her ghostly chest when she saw his familiar stride. It didn't matter that he wore the same uniform every day. Somehow, he seemed to look more handsome each time she saw him. His white button-down shirt showed off his masculine physique so perfectly.

"This is my favorite spot to sit when the weather's good," Gregory said as he approached her. He sat down next to her in the shade.

"I know," she said.

"Have you watched me eat lunch here before?"

"I've seen you sitting here a lot during my travels during the day, that's all," Rebekah replied honestly. Until now, she hadn't joined him for lunch. She had watched him from afar though. It made her happy to see him taking a break during his workday.

"How's your blood sugar?" she asked as she watched him unwrap his sandwich.

"Good. Checked it before I left the shop."

"Glad to hear it," she said. Rebekah worried about Gregory's health after what had happened that terrible day. She waited to speak again until he'd had a chance to eat a few bites of his sandwich, just to make sure he was all right.

Looking out at the leaves on the trees softly rustling in the breeze, she said, "It's such a beautiful day. I can tell by the way people are dressed that it's not too hot or too cold."

She recalled how pleasant the month of May was in Virginia when she was alive.

"You're right. It's the perfect temperature right now," Gregory said. "I wish you could feel it."

"Me too," Rebekah said, though she'd learned long ago

not to dwell on all the things she missed about being alive. It was pointless.

Gregory closed his eyes and drew in a breath, then slowly let it out. "Being with you is certainly a reminder not to take things for granted."

"Gregory," she said, her tone suddenly serious.

He nodded, looking concerned.

"I want you to know how happy I am to have you as my friend. I really can't tell you how much it means to me."

Gregory smiled, the warmth spreading all the way to his eyes. "I feel the same way."

Rebekah felt unsure. He probably had lots of friends already. *Living* friends who could eat and drink and go places with him. She must be rather dull in comparison.

"No, I mean it," he insisted. Thoughtfully, he took a bite of his sandwich and then took a sip from his bottle of unsweetened tea. He paused after he finished his mouthful, as if he wasn't sure how much he wanted to say. "I'm still kind of feeling my way around here. I don't know a lot of people in Virginia, and it's pretty far from my family."

"Where are they?"

"Florida," he said, still seeming hesitant.

"Will you tell me about your family?"

"Sure. In addition to my parents, I have an older sister and a younger brother. My sister's married and my brother's single."

Gregory paused again. Rebekah waited.

"And I had a wife."

"You were married?" Rebekah asked, astonished. The vision of Gregory wearing a tuxedo and standing at the altar with a woman wearing a beautiful white wedding gown nearly tore her heart to pieces. Stupid as it was, she frequently daydreamed about marrying Gregory herself.

Rebekah might no longer have a physical body, but the sharp pain she felt was incredibly physical.

Married. Gregory had been married.

He'd had a courtship and a wedding and a honeymoon. And a wedding night. Naturally, Rebekah had assumed that Gregory had made love to other women, but she'd never allowed herself to think much about it. Now she was forced to confront the truth.

It took all the strength she could muster to hide her heartbreak.

"Oh. I didn't know," she forced herself to say.

Gregory's somber expression made her realize how selfish she was being. He said he'd *had* a wife. My God, what if she'd died in a horrible accident? Or perhaps succumbed to some terrible illness? The ache in her chest grew as she contemplated his pain. Thinking of his suffering was far worse than dwelling on her own.

He studied the grass instead of looking at Rebekah. "Now *ex*-wife. I'm pretty recently divorced, and I moved up here from Florida to try to make a fresh start."

"Oh, I see," Rebekah said, her emotions swirling inside of her. She was relieved to know Gregory's wife hadn't died tragically. But maybe she had left him for another man or something. How awful. "You're so young to be divorced. I'm sorry."

"Thanks. I appreciate it."

"May I ask what happened?" Rebekah asked, her curiosity getting the best of her.

Gregory laughed ruefully. "What happened? Now, that's a good question."

"You don't have to answer if you don't want to."

"No, it's okay. I guess I wouldn't have brought it up if I

didn't want to talk about it." He paused to gather his thoughts. "Nothing. Nothing really happened."

He shook his head sorrowfully.

"It's strange," Gregory continued. "I think it would have been much easier if something had happened. Like if she cheated on me, or left me for another guy, or something. But it was nothing like that."

He paused for a long time. Rebekah was about to say something to encourage him to go on, but he spoke again before she could say anything.

"I'm sorry. I've never been able to explain the situation very well. At least not in a way that anybody seems to understand."

"Try me," Rebekah said. "Maybe I will understand."

Gregory smiled, seeming encouraged by her words.

"It just didn't ... my marriage didn't ..." He faltered, and Rebekah could hear the frustration in his voice. "It didn't feel the way I thought it would. God, that sounds so stupid!"

"No, it doesn't. Try to explain what you mean. And what you're feeling. Don't overthink it. Tell me what's on your mind and in your heart. Don't worry about me judging you, because I'm not."

The deep gratitude she saw in his eyes tugged at her heart. She could see how badly he needed to get this burden off his chest.

"Vanessa and I got together in the last year of high school and dated all through college and beyond," he said, his words flowing much more rapidly and freely now. "We were together all the time, and we loved each other very much. We both wanted to settle down and raise a family, and after all those years of dating, it seemed like the right thing to do. She's a wonderful woman, and everybody was always saying how perfect we were for each other. We were like one of those couples everybody aspires to be. Gregory and Vanessa, together forever. Everybody said we'd make it to our 50th anniversary, you know?"

Rebekah listened intently, careful not to make a sound. She didn't want to interrupt Gregory as he poured his heart out, and she didn't want him to second-guess his decision to confide in her.

"I loved her very much, and I honestly didn't have a clue that it wasn't going to work out. Not even at our wedding. Nobody did."

He paused again, and Rebekah nodded in understanding and sympathy.

"On paper, it was perfect. We got along great, and it seemed we both wanted the same things. I don't know. I guess I *did* know all along that, as much as I loved her, I wasn't passionate about her. That, and we did have our differences."

"Like what?" Rebekah asked after Gregory seemed hesitant.

"Well, for one, she really likes to go out and party on the weekend. You know, drinking and going to clubs. That's not my speed. Besides, I can't drink much alcohol because of my health issues. God, she must have been so bored with me, but she never said it."

"She sounds a little immature."

Gregory thought that over for a moment. "It does sound like she's immature, doesn't it? But she really isn't. I mean, she likes to go out and party and drink, but she was never irresponsible. She would never drive drunk, and she has a steady job, and she's reliable and all that. She just likes to have a good time. Vanessa is the life of the party wherever she goes."

The ache in Rebekah's chest grew stronger again when

she heard the pride in Gregory's voice when he spoke about his ex-wife.

"Vanessa is full of energy and passion and enthusiasm. I'm nothing like that, and I don't think I ever knew what she saw in me. But she loved me. She still loves me. That's the worst part. God, I never meant to hurt her."

Gregory closed his eyes, and Rebekah wished she could put her arms around him to comfort him.

"She didn't know why I wanted a divorce, and I hate like hell that I put her through that. Vanessa didn't understand. Nobody understood. I know it sounds incredibly stupid. Like I said, I can't really explain. All I know is that I was unhappy, and that being married to Vanessa wasn't what I expected. I guess deep down I knew that being in love wasn't supposed to be like this. It was supposed to feel ... different, somehow. I don't know. Maybe I'm crazy. Maybe this is just what love is."

"I don't think so."

"Really?"

"If it doesn't feel right, then it isn't right. Even if it's hard to explain why."

Gregory paused thoughtfully. "All I know is, yeah, it didn't feel right. I kept waiting for things to get better, for me to feel better, but I didn't. And then she started talking about having kids, and I knew I couldn't do it." His jaw hardened. "Knowing that there was even a possibility we'd get divorced."

"That was a wise decision."

"Yes," Gregory said with a sigh. "I think so too. So, I came out here to Williamsburg to kind of get my head on straight."

"Is it working?"

"Depends on the day," he said. "Usually. Yeah. Yeah, I

think it has helped to get away and have time to think. Most people around here don't know much about my past, so I never have to talk about it."

"Until now," Rebekah said.

"Yeah. But it's okay."

They sat in comfortable silence for a few moments. Rebekah watched him carefully, noticing he was lost in thought.

"What are you thinking about?" she asked.

"There was this one time I was playing piano at home. I play all the time."

"Nice," Rebekah said, easily picturing Gregory joyously pounding away at the keys, filling the house with beautiful music.

"And Vanessa came into the room while I was playing. I really get into it, you know? Like, I just get lost in the music."

"I know you do," she said. She adored the way he looked while playing the harpsichord. His brown hair whipping around in his face, his head dramatically bobbing along with the music.

Sexy. That was the only way to describe the way he looked when he played.

"So, I'm playing one of my favorite songs and getting really into it. Music is so cathartic for me. It's such a rush and release all at once. Anyway, I'm playing away, and Vanessa comes in to tell me dinner's ready. Ugh, listen to me. Complaining about my wife who made me this wonderful dinner. Just hearing myself say this out loud makes me realize how ungrateful I am."

"Don't you worry about that. Just say what you want to say. Stop second-guessing yourself and tell me what you're feeling."

"I wanted her to listen to me," he said bluntly. Rebekah

nodded silently, urging him to continue. "Vanessa never complained about me playing the piano or anything. She never made fun of me or told me I was wasting my time and should be doing chores around the house. She always tolerated my playing. That night, she patiently waited for me to finish my song and then told me dinner was ready."

Rebekah understood exactly what he was trying to say.

"And what do you wish she had done?"

"I wanted her to *listen*," Gregory said earnestly. "I always had this picture in my head of marriage. I imagined my wife hearing me play music and then coming in the room to watch. She'd stand in the doorway, leaning against the frame, and just watch me play and listen to my song. And then when I was done, she would tell me how beautiful it was."

He laughed uncomfortably and looked away.

"I know it sounds so dumb, but—"

"No!" she insisted. "It doesn't sound dumb at *all*. A man deserves a wife who is proud of him. A woman who knows him best and loves him for who he is, and especially loves the best parts of him. Music is such a part of you. Who you are. Part of your *soul*. I can see that when you play. I've always seen it. The way your eyes light up, and the way you play with such intensity," she said, pantomiming his dramatic hand motions. "I love it, Gregory. I love to watch you play, and it's not because I'm bored and I have nothing else to do. I come to the shop almost every day, hoping to hear you play."

He met her gaze. She saw so much in his eyes. Gratitude, warmth, and maybe even affection.

"I understand, Gregory. I really do."

"Thank you." Simple words, but she could hear the relief in them. "And I mean, don't get me wrong, I wanted to do the same for her. And I did. At least I hope I did. I was proud of her. I *am* proud of her. She's amazing. Warm, funny, and kind. Fearless on the dance floor. Brave, ambitious …"

Rebekah's smile froze, and she tried to ignore the searing pain of jealousy and sorrow at hearing him heap praise and admiration on another woman.

He laughed suddenly, and then said, "Vanessa is an incredible woman, but when it comes down to it, my wife just wasn't my type."

Rebekah laughed, too. From what he had described, it was true. It occurred to Rebekah that for Gregory, being married to Vanessa would be like Rebekah being married to Orlando. Orlando was a wonderful man. Quite talented, outrageous, funny, and kind. Rebekah was fond of him, but not as a husband. It would be a terrible fit.

"You did the right thing in getting divorced. I know it's incredibly painful and sad, but it was the right thing to do."

"Nobody understands," he said. "My parents try to support me in anything I do, but they just didn't get it. They adore Vanessa. They thought we would give them grandkids. They thought she and I would grow old together."

"Do you miss her?"

"No."

"Then that's really all you need to know, now isn't it?"

"I guess."

"I'm not saying it's easy, Gregory. But doing the right thing rarely is."

"How'd you get so wise?"

"I'm over two hundred and fifty years old," she said. He laughed, which warmed her heart.

"I hate to say it, but I have to get back to work."

"I know." Rebekah's heart felt heavy at the thought of him leaving.

Gregory leaned in toward her and said softly, "I'll see you again soon, okay?"

She nodded.

"Hey there, kids!" came a booming voice from nearby.

They turned to see Orlando walking by with another man dressed in a colonial outfit, wig, and tricorn hat. Orlando raised a curious eyebrow at the two of them as he walked on.

Rebekah couldn't contain her smile. Orlando clearly thought there was something going on between her and Gregory, and she loved it. Having anyone think she was Gregory's girlfriend made her practically giddy. She couldn't get over how jealous he had seemed when Orlando had harmlessly flirted with her.

Gregory sighed heavily. "I really have to get going. Rebekah, thank you for listening to me."

"Thank you for treating me like a friend instead of a dead woman."

"I like to think we'd be more than friends if that were possible."

Rebekah felt the physical sensation of her throat tightening, as if she were on the verge of tears. "D—do you really mean that?"

"Yes. In case you hadn't noticed, I'm kinda crazy about you."

"I feel the same way," she said, allowing herself to gaze longingly into his eyes. After so long, she finally felt as if she had permission to openly adore him.

"Well, I confided a bunch of stuff about my personal life to you. Maybe sometime soon you'll trust me enough to do the same?" he asked hopefully.

Rebekah winced at the thought. There were things about her past she didn't want Gregory to know. Ever.

"Like maybe tell me why you're still here, so I can try to help you get to where you're supposed to be?"

She remained silent.

"Just think about it, okay?"

Rebekah nodded, an uneasy feeling stirring in her ghostly stomach.

11

As Gregory stood in a light rain waiting for the bus to take him back to the Visitor Center at the end of the day, he reflected on his conversation with Rebekah. He marveled at how she seemed to understand him so well, right from the beginning. He'd first noticed it when she came to see him that day on the bridge behind the shop. At his mention that he loved music, she'd replied softly, *I know.*

Right then, Gregory had felt a strong connection with her. Something in the way she looked at him and the way she really listened to him made him feel she understood him in a way nobody else ever had.

And there was the way Rebekah had stood beside him as he played the harpsichord. Sure, she was a ghost and had nowhere else to go and nothing to do, but it was more than that. She was touched by the sound of the music. He could see it in her eyes. When he explained that his wife didn't seem to get how much music meant to him, Rebekah had understood.

"I hate what this damn humidity does to my powdered

wig." Orlando sniffed as he patted down his fake hair. Gregory had been so lost in thought, he hadn't noticed Orlando sidling up to him at the bus stop.

Gregory chuckled. "Yeah, I hate that."

"So, what's with you and the pretty brunette? She new around here?"

Gregory laughed harder than he should have at that. "No. No, she's not new."

"Quite a dish, that one."

"Yeah, she is. She's also very sweet."

"Cool," Orlando said.

"She's unavailable, though," he said somberly.

"Married?"

"No. No, she's not married."

"Well, then maybe she's only temporarily unavailable. Look, I'm not sayin' you should swoop in on another guy's girl, but if it's meant to be, it's meant to be."

"Yeah," Gregory said, knowing for sure it was *not* meant to be.

The bus arrived, and Gregory, Orlando, and a handful of tourists got on board. Orlando sat in a seat directly across from Gregory.

"Can I ask you a question?" Gregory asked.

"Shoot."

"Orlando's not your real name, is it?"

He chuckled and shook his head. "No, no it's not." Lowering his voice, he said with a grimace, "My real name's Gordon."

"That name does *not* suit you."

"Thanks. I take that as a compliment. It's a family name. My dad wanted it for me. My mom hated it. Dad won."

"So, did you pick Orlando as a stage name? Did you get it from Shakespeare?"

"It is from Shakespeare, and yeah, I guess it is a stage name of sorts. I mean, I do use it as my real name now outside of work, too. I had it legally changed."

Orlando got quiet for a moment.

"The name's from Shakespeare's *As You Like It*. It was my mom's idea. She wanted to name me Orlando when I was born. It's funny, ya know? It was like she knew I was gonna be an actor. So I changed my name to Orlando when she died."

"Oh, man, I didn't know you lost your mom. I'm so sorry."

"Thanks," Orlando said, and Gregory could see the deep sorrow in his eyes. "Drunk driver hit her car head on. I was seven."

"Jesus."

"Yeah. Sucks," he said with a rueful laugh.

"Well, changing your name was a great way to honor her."

"Thanks," Orlando said with a smile. "I think so too."

The bus arrived at the Visitor Center, and everyone filed off.

"See ya later," Orlando called. "And don't give up on … What's her name?"

"Rebekah," Gregory said. He could hear the reverence in his own voice as he said her name.

"Rebekah. Don't give up on her. You guys'd be great together."

Gregory nodded.

"Yeah. I know."

∽

Rebekah stood on the bridge behind the shop, waiting for Gregory. She glanced up and smiled when he came outside. His heart thumped and a ripple of pleasure went through his body. She was so lovely, and there was nothing prettier than her smile.

They had agreed to meet after work this time, both because Ben was working with Gregory, and to give them a chance to get out of the shop for a while. They couldn't exactly go on a date, but they didn't have to stay inside Hay's all the time, either.

"Did you—" she began.

"Yes, I had something to eat. I'm good," Gregory said with a grin. He'd promised he would grab a snack before they met up at the end of the day.

She smiled again, warming his heart all over again.

"Where would you like to go?" Gregory asked.

"Do you want to see where I used to live? I mean, I'm sure you've seen it before."

"Yeah, I have. But not with you. Sure, I'd love to go see Jennings Tavern with you."

They walked together down Nicholson Street, and then down Botetourt Street toward Jennings Tavern on Duke of Gloucester Street. It was a nice night, warm but not too hot. The crowds had thinned a little, since most of the buildings were closing.

Gregory drew in a deep breath of fresh air, having learned from Rebekah's plight not to take things like breathing for granted. He caught the familiar scent of smoked meat in the air from one of the nearby taverns serving dinner. He also noticed the cool breeze on his face and through his hair. So many things Rebekah had to miss out on.

"You all right?" Rebekah asked.

"Oh, yeah. I'm just thinking."

"What are you thinking about?"

Vanessa never asked me that.

"Just how nice the weather is, and how everything smells so good around here, and I wish you could enjoy those things."

Rebekah smiled, making his heart flutter again. "That's very sweet. You get used to it, believe me. It's okay. I can see the leaves on the trees and watch them sway in the wind. I can watch the sun set every night, and watch the kids run around and play their little tin whistles."

Gregory chuckled. "Yeah."

"In my state, you really do learn to appreciate the little things. After all, life—and in my case, even death—is made up of millions of little moments. That's why it was important to you that your wife stop and listen to you play your music. Little moments like that really aren't little after all."

"That's the truth," Gregory said. "So, I asked Orlando about his name."

"Really? And did he tell you everything?"

"Yeah," he said somberly. "I had no idea his mother had died."

"Oh," Rebekah said, placing her hand near her heart. "I know. It's so tragic. He was just a little boy. You always need your mother, but never more than when you're a child."

As they got within eyesight of Jennings Tavern, Gregory watched Rebekah's face. She brightened when she saw the building, but her eyes showed a hint of wistfulness and sorrow.

"I'm sorry we can't go in now," she said. "Well *I* can. But I'm sure the door's locked. I guess you've been in there before?"

Jennings Tavern wasn't a working restaurant like some of

the other taverns in the area. Rather, it had been restored to look much like it had in the 1700s and was open for tourists to come in and visit like they did with the cabinetmaker's shop.

"Yeah, I have. I've visited pretty much all of the buildings at one time or another. I can't say I remember exactly what it looks like inside. Plenty to see outside, though."

Except for a few stragglers walking down the street, they were mostly alone. They paused in front of the large white building with green shutters. The Jennings Tavern sign creaked as it swung slightly in the breeze. Gregory counted fourteen windows on the top and bottom of the house. There were several rooms for guests, plus Rebekah's entire family had lived there. Gregory realized the Jennings family must have been fairly wealthy.

She approached one of the windows, and he followed her.

"This was the public dining room," she explained, peering in the window. She stepped back to let him have a look.

The first thing Gregory noticed was the big wooden table located in the center of the room. He couldn't help admiring the craftsmanship, considering what he did for a living. The chairs were also finely crafted, and he took particular note of the designs on the chair legs.

"Nice furniture," he said.

"Yes. You should know. You're the expert," Rebekah said. Gregory rather liked being called an expert, since he was quite proud of the work he did in the shop.

Rebekah walked over to the next window. "In here is what we called the Great Room. This is where businessmen and travelers would meet to talk about all sorts of interesting things. They'd discuss the places they'd visited and about politics and business. I can't say I always understood everything they were talking about, but I confess I absolutely loved to listen in on their conversations."

Her pretty eyes flashed with mischief, and Gregory grinned at her. She stepped aside to allow him to look inside. It was a large room with a wooden floor and a bunch of chairs pushed against the walls. Gregory assumed it was set up that way to allow a large tour group to enter as they listened to the tavern host tell them the history of Jennings Tavern.

"The business meetings were fascinating, but best of all was when we had wedding receptions here. Oh, I loved that!" Rebekah gushed, eyes shining. "To see everyone dressed up so fancy. The bride always looked beautiful. That was my favorite part. Seeing what the bride wore, because it was always something lovely. Brides didn't wear white back then like they do now. They wore beautiful dresses, though. Ones with lots of color and lovely detail. Oh, I *really* love the fancy wedding gowns they wear today!"

Gregory chuckled at Rebekah's enthusiasm. "You are *such* a girly-girl."

She laughed happily. "I am. I really am."

"I think it's cute," he told her. Her pretty smile broadened. "So, I guess you never married?"

Rebekah shook her head, her expression falling. "No. I never got the chance."

It wasn't surprising that she had been unmarried when she died, since most women got married in their early to mid-twenties back then. As always, burning questions about her death were on the tip of his tongue, but he resisted the urge to ask. She seemed so happy showing him where she had lived, and he didn't want to put a damper on that. Besides, if she wanted to talk about it, she would.

"This next one here is another meeting room," she explained as Gregory peered inside. This room had a gorgeous mahogany desk and a wooden clock.

"Very nice. I'm gonna have to go on the tour of the building again so I can get a closer look inside."

"And upstairs, in addition to the rooms where my family slept, were all the sleeping places for the guests," she said.

Gregory knew why Rebekah said "sleeping places" instead of bedrooms. It was common in the 1700s to share a bedroom, or even a bed, with other travelers. Since it was almost always men who traveled alone, it wasn't considered a big deal to share a bed with somebody you didn't know.

"Then, of course, there's all the buildings around the back. Come on," she said, gesturing.

He followed her into a small, wooden outbuilding behind the main Jennings Tavern building. Gregory was happy to see that the smile had returned to her face. This was the kitchen, set up to look just as it would have when she was alive. There was a large fireplace built into the stone wall, with a big black cauldron resting inside, as if waiting for someone to cook a meal. Metal spoons and other cooking utensils hung on hooks on the wall next to the fireplace. Metal pots and pans adorned the walls.

"I loved our kitchen. I used to cook and bake lots of things."

"Like gingerbread."

"Yes!" Rebekah said with excitement in her eyes. It occurred to Gregory that it had probably been a long time since anyone had asked her anything about her personal life. Maybe hundreds of years. *Mind-boggling.*

"You cannot imagine how hot it got in here on a summer day," Rebekah said as she walked around the tiny kitchen.

"Wow. No. I really can't imagine," he marveled. The heat

in Virginia could be positively stifling in the summer, and it was beyond him how anyone could possibly cook over an open flame in July and August.

After they finished looking around, they walked out of the kitchen and over to the next building. "That's just the smokehouse."

Rebekah paused for a moment as she gazed at the next set of wooden buildings. Gregory understood her hesitation.

Those buildings were the slaves' quarters.

"And this here is where the slaves slept," she said quietly. "They were back here so as to be kept away from the gentlemen travelers and parties and everything going on in the house. Like a dirty little secret."

There was a hard edge to Rebekah's voice as she spoke.

"Did it upset you that your family owned slaves?" Gregory asked.

"I wish I could tell you that it did," she responded, looking down. "It upsets me now. A lot. But back then, no. I didn't have much objection to it."

He nodded, taking in her words and doing his best to understand.

The slaves' quarters were no more than run-down shacks and not much bigger than the kitchen and smokehouse.

"My God, what were we thinking?" she whispered. She turned to him, her eyes pleading with him to understand. "It was such a different time in those days. Not that it makes it right. Of course not. It's just ..."

"Just tell me what you're thinking and feeling. I'm not judging you," Gregory said, remembering how comforting and encouraging those words had been when she said them.

"Oh, it just sounds too awful to 21st-century ears! But we

were told they were just like animals," she said, wincing. "We were brought up to believe they were not like us. That it didn't hurt them to be slaves. That they were better off for having someone put a roof over their head and tell them what to do."

She shook her head in disgust, which made Gregory feel better. He did his best not to judge Rebekah and her family for what they did in the past, but it wasn't easy. How could anyone have thought it was okay to own human beings like property?

"I know it seems so strange, but when it's your family telling you these things, you don't really question it. My mother and father taught me from the time I was a little girl that black people were not like us. When you're little, you believe everything your parents tell you, don't you?"

"That's true."

"And, of course, it wasn't just my family. That's just the way it was for everyone back then. And I believed it was all right. Although ..."

He waited patiently for her to continue.

"There was a time when I was working in the kitchen, baking as usual. One of the slave women was helping me. Dorothy. It was a normal day, and she was kneading the dough for bread, and I just caught her eye. It was no big deal, but for some reason looking her in the eye really struck me. Looking in her eyes, I could see ..."

"What?" Gregory asked, intrigued.

"Her humanity," she said, her voice nearly a whisper. "In that moment, I was suddenly full of uncertainty. I clearly remember thinking, what if we're wrong? What if black people are no different from us? What if they're exactly the same as us except for the color of their skin? The idea was almost too horrible to contemplate. If the slaves were just like us, then they must be suffering terribly, and what we were doing to them was horrible."

Rebekah gazed sadly at the wooden slave shacks that were barely fit to house animals, let alone human beings.

"But then I kept thinking about everything I was taught by my parents and everybody else. I suppose I figured they knew best, so I put the idea out of my head. Just another horrible thing I've done in my life."

Gregory heard the anger and bitterness in her voice.

She walked up to one of the slave shacks and peered inside for a moment. Gregory stayed where he was, allowing her to have a quiet moment with her thoughts. Then she turned and walked toward the front of the tavern, and he followed her.

When they reached the front lawn, she asked, "Why don't we sit for a while? You must be tired of standing."

He nodded, and they sat together on the front lawn of the Jennings Tavern. A few people walked by and smiled at them, admiring Gregory's costume and Rebekah's real 18th-century clothing. She really did blend in perfectly here.

"So, you mentioned a brother and sister, right?" he asked.

"Yes. My sister, Martha, was a few years older, and my brother, Nathaniel, was much younger," Rebekah said. "My parents were nearly past the child-bearing age. Nathaniel was a surprise to my parents I believe."

Gregory chuckled. "What they call a 'change of life' baby."

"Oh, he was a surprise to all of us, but we all loved him dearly. He was a bright-eyed little boy with brown eyes and light blond hair," she said fondly as she spoke of her baby brother. "Nathaniel was curious about everything. Talked,

talked, talked all the time! And he asked a thousand questions every day."

"He sounds adorable."

"He was," Rebekah said. "Oh, he was. I adored him. I simply *adored* him."

"How old was he when you died?"

"Three."

"That must have been hard for your family. Tough to explain death to a three-year-old."

Her sweet face broke for a moment, and she looked down. Her lip trembled, like she was trying not to cry.

"I'm sorry, Rebekah. I didn't mean to upset you," Gregory said. He desperately wanted to wrap his arms around her.

"It's okay," she said shakily. He was struck by the deep pain in her eyes. He couldn't begin to imagine how badly she missed her family.

"Of course, I adored my older sister too. She was so pretty. I wanted to be just like her," Rebekah said, the smile returning to her face. "She had the most beautiful wavy hair. We shared a room until she got married and moved to a small house with her husband, Philip. Oh, he was so handsome. I couldn't help but be jealous of Martha for having such a dashing man in her life."

She seemed lost in her memories.

Laughing softly, she said, "I remember a time, not long after they got married, I went to visit them in their new house. I had baked some sweets for them. When I got to their place, I heard noises from inside. I confess that I ..." She looked down shyly. "I—I stood outside for a while and just ... listened ..."

It took Gregory a moment to understand what she was saying. Finally, he got it.

"Oh. You mean, they were ..."

"Yes," she said, laughing nervously and continuing to avoid looking at him. "They were newlyweds after all. I've never told anyone about this before. I just ... I guess I just wanted to know ..."

"It's natural to be curious, Rebekah," Gregory said, quite amused at her confession. She still wouldn't meet his gaze. "I have a feeling that if you still had blood in you, you'd be blushing right now."

Smiling sweetly, she finally lifted her gaze to his. "I believe you're right."

"And what did you learn?" he asked.

"It sounded like fun."

Gregory chuckled, and she laughed along with him.

"My goodness. I've never spoken about such a thing aloud before!"

Charmed by her bashful confession, he gazed at her lovely features. He half-expected her to fan her face from the embarrassment.

After a moment, she added dreamily, "I can't imagine how romantic it would be to have a loving husband to do that with."

"I guess you were never, you know, with a man?" he asked.

"No. But I always wanted to be," she confessed. With that, she turned to look him right in the eye. He wondered if she would have let him make love to her if she were still alive.

"I couldn't help being sweet on Philip for a while. He was older than me and so *manly*. After a while, he became more like a big brother to me. He was a good man. And he was a good father to their children."

"You miss him," Gregory said, noting the sadness in her tone.

"Yes. I miss all of them," Rebekah said with a noticeable hitch in her voice. "No matter how long it's been, you never forget the people you love."

"You'll see them again."

After a moment of silence, she said, "I love being with you, Gregory."

His face broke into a huge grin. "I love being with you, too."

"You're so easy to talk to. I love that you're calm and quiet."

Gregory shook his head upon hearing that.

"What?"

"My wife used to say I was maddeningly calm."

"It's not a bad thing," Rebekah reassured him.

"Vanessa was very sociable. It's funny. People think I'm introverted, but I'm really not. I enjoy being around people. I'm just kinda low key. She was more excitable, and I think it bothered her that I wasn't. We didn't fight a lot, but when we did, I never got all worked up like she did. I think that annoyed her."

"How strange," she said. "I like that you're calm. It helps me feel calm. More at peace. When I'm with you, my thoughts quiet down a bit. Being alone a lot, I tend to ruminate and obsess over everything I've ever done wrong in my life. When you sit and talk with me, the madness in my head stops for a while."

"I'm glad," Gregory said. "I like that we can do simple things together, like walk around Williamsburg and just be happy."

"Me too."

"Not that I wouldn't love to take you out somewhere if it were possible. I would. It's just I feel like I could sit around the house with you and be content."

"I feel the same way," Rebekah said, gracing him with one of those smiles that set his heart to racing. "I doubt I would have been into the club scene, even if there had been such a thing when I was alive."

"Now how do you know about stuff like the club scene?" Gregory asked. The historical setting in the area was quite well-preserved. Though there probably were nightclubs somewhere in Williamsburg, they were nowhere near here.

"Television," she answered simply. "Sometimes I sit and watch when people have the TV on. I've learned a lot that way."

"Where?"

"Nearby hotels. The dorms at the College of William and Mary. Places like that."

"Wow," he marveled. There were so many things a ghost could do that had never occurred to him. "Forget just listening. I can't imagine all the things you might *see* while hanging out in a hotel room."

Rebekah's eyes flew open wide. "Gregory! I would never ... w—w—watch such a thing!"

He laughed. She was so cute when she was flustered. "I know, I know. You're a lady."

"Yes, I am," she said primly, but he could see the glint of mischief in her eyes. He believed she would never watch couples having sex in hotel rooms, but he also knew she was curious about it. How he would have loved to satisfy her curiosity himself.

She eyed him suspiciously, as if she was aware of his naughty thoughts. At first, he worried she was angry, but then she started laughing and he joined in. He felt good all over just being near her.

"Anyway," she said sternly, with the twinkle still in her eye, "though I would have no interest in the loud nightclub scene, I would *love* to go dancing. I remember watching all those glamorous ladies dancing with their gentlemen when we hosted parties at the tavern. I always dreamed of dancing with a man like that."

"I guess that's another thing you never got to do, huh?"

"No, I never did," she said, her voiced filled with regret.

It was nearly quarter 'til eight, and the sun was setting.

"So beautiful," Rebekah said. "I've seen a lot of sunsets in my time, and they're always beautiful."

Gregory watched her as she watched the sun setting in a burst of colors through the clouds. "Not nearly as beautiful as you are."

She turned to look at him, eyes filled with gratitude at his words.

"Now would be the perfect time to kiss you," he said.

"Yes," she whispered. He could see the longing in her eyes, and he wondered if she'd ever been kissed before. He reached over and pressed his fingers to her lips.

"Does it feel cold?" she asked.

Gregory nodded. She smiled sadly.

"You still won't tell me," he said.

"Tell you what?"

"Why you're here."

Rebekah looked away.

"'Oh while you live, tell the truth and shame the devil,'" he said, quoting Shakespeare.

A smile crept into the corners of her mouth, and he knew she'd recognized the quote.

"Though I would miss you terribly if you crossed over, I want you to be happy and at peace, Rebekah. I know there are things you don't want to tell me. Stuff you don't want to talk about, but it might help you."

She gazed sorrowfully into his eyes.

"It's getting dark. You need to go home and get some rest." With that, she stood up.

Gregory stood, too, and they walked toward the bus that would take him to the Visitor Center parking lot. When they reached the bus stop, no one else was there.

"I had a wonderful evening with you. Thank you."

Rebekah smiled gratefully up at him. She glanced around to make sure no one else was watching, and then she disappeared.

12

Gregory lay in bed staring at the ceiling and thinking about Rebekah. He had never felt so connected to any other human being, living or dead. Their discussions about music and Shakespeare, their families, and even their moments of silence drew him to her. Made him feel comfortable. Safe. Happy. Attracted. Aroused. All the things you feel when you meet the right person. When you meet your ...

Soulmate.

Could there be a word that better described his situation with Rebekah? Her soul was literally all that she had left, and that was what he felt connected to.

If things were different, he'd probably be telling his family and friends all about this wonderful girl he'd met. But things weren't different. They were what they were. He was alive. She was dead. There was no changing that.

Gregory rolled over onto his side and looked at the empty spot next to him. It was strange how he really didn't miss Vanessa. How that spot next to him hadn't really felt empty, even in the early days after his divorce. But now it did seem empty. It was so easy to imagine Rebekah lying next to him, as if she was supposed to be here with him, and yet she wasn't.

And she never would be.

∽

Gregory and Rebekah made arrangements to meet again the next evening. He had eaten a hasty sandwich for dinner after work so they could go walking together. He loved spending as much time with her as possible. Every minute seemed precious, since it was impossible to know how much time they would have together.

He supposed that was true of everyone. No matter what the circumstance, no one knew how much time they had to spend with the people they cared about. Rebekah's family had probably had no idea that the last time they spoke to her would be the last time they saw her alive.

What happened to you, Rebekah?

Gregory locked the door to the shop and, as always, his heart lurched in his chest when he saw Rebekah waiting for him.

"You're so beautiful," he told her.

"You don't know how much I wish I could change my clothes. Dress up for you."

"I think you look lovely," he told her. "And it's not like you ever get to see me wearing anything different. I'm always in my work uniform."

"And what a handsome uniform it is," Rebekah said as she looked him up and down.

He smiled down at her; he was at least a head taller than her. Once again, this would be another perfect time to kiss her. Gregory had never realized how much he'd taken the sense of touch for granted.

They began walking together, falling into step comfortably.

"How was your day?" she asked.

A lump suddenly formed in his throat. It was such a normal, ordinary question. Just as it had been easy to imagine Rebekah lying beside him in bed, he could easily imagine her greeting him each day when he got home from work. *Honey, how was your day?*

"Gregory?" she asked, sounding worried.

"Oh, sorry. Good. It was a good day."

"I'm glad to hear it," she said.

After walking down the street a ways, Rebekah asked, "Do you want to sit?" gesturing toward a bench facing Bruton Parish Church, outside the brick building with the ticket office.

"Sure."

She smiled as she sat down, or at least appeared to sit down, on the bench. "I like people-watching with you."

Together, they sat and watched tourists go by. Families and couples. Gregory watched enviously as a man walked down the street with his arm around a woman. Such a simple gesture, and yet something he could never do with Rebekah.

"It's okay if you ever have plans in the evening, you know. I feel bad keeping you here after work all the time," she said.

"There's no place I'd rather be than with you," Gregory said.

"What did you do in the evenings before you got stuck hanging out with me?"

"Well, I would hardly call this being stuck with you," he

said, gazing into her eyes. He took his time admiring her for a moment before speaking again. "I usually just ate dinner by myself in front of the TV."

"Oh," she said, looking somber. It did sound lonely when he said it out loud, but it really hadn't bothered him much. After spending so much time stressing out over the divorce, it was a relief to be by himself for a while. Being with Vanessa every night had filled him with dread and uncertainty about the future as he agonized about whether or not he should end his marriage. Having peaceful dinners while watching mindless television was much easier.

"It's not as bad as it sounds. Sometimes after dinner I'd play music."

"Piano?" she asked, her eyes lighting up.

"Yeah," Gregory said. As usual, she seemed interested in his music. Rebekah would have stood in the doorway of his apartment and listened to him play. He was sure of it.

"What did you used to do in the evenings? I mean, not now. Like, before. When you were ..."

"Breathing?" she said.

"Yeah. That."

"Well, sometimes I would help prepare dinner, and then eat with the family. It was quite a lot of work back then to make meals. Not like now where even when you're making a meal from scratch, it doesn't take that long. It wasn't like we would prepare and cook food for an hour before dinner and be done with it. Depending on what you were making, it could take hours. Days, even!"

Gregory watched Rebekah, enjoying the happy look in her eyes as she spoke. She clearly had many fond memories of her life, and he was fascinated to hear firsthand about life in the 1700s.

"Especially if you were making cheese. I absolutely *love*

cheese, but you can't imagine how much work it is to make. You had to get the fire ready to get the milk to curdle, and then break the curds in the cheese press by placing them on the cheese-ladder and turn them constantly. You know The Cheese Shop, right? On Merchants Square?"

Gregory nodded. Merchants Square was a shopping plaza full of souvenir shops and restaurants. It was located not far from the College of William and Mary, outside the historical district.

Rebekah shook her head. "Sometimes I walk through there just to see what they have. Unbelievable how many varieties of cheese they have there from all over the world. Even after all these years, I still marvel about how much time it would take to make all that cheese back in my day. Everything was a lot of work back then, but I liked being busy. That's one of the hardest things about being the way I am now. I can't do much of anything. When I was—"

She stopped herself before saying *when I was alive*. There were too many people around for that kind of honesty. She could sit and talk about life in the 1700s all day, especially dressed the way she was. People just assumed she was in character. But being dead was another story.

"Back then, there was always so much to do. Cooking and baking, and making clothing, making candles. Of course ..."

Gregory eyed her curiously as she trailed off.

"Slaves did most of that work," she said with a wince. "I baked a lot because I enjoyed it. Not because I had to, like they did. I was lucky. I had plenty of time to do embroidery, and I loved to read. And then in the evening, I got to sit down to dinner with my family. It was wonderful. And then in the evenings after supper, I would ..."

She trailed off again, looking sorrowful.

"You would..." he prompted.

"Sing," she said weakly. "I would sing songs for the family. We had a harpsichord, though it wasn't as beautiful as the one you made."

"Did you play it?"

"No, I never learned how. My father played it, and I sang. My little brother especially loved when I sang. I made up little songs just for him."

"Cute," Gregory said, imagining Rebekah's tiny three-year-old brother bouncing around as she sang to him. It was clear how much Rebekah adored her baby brother. Her eyes took on such gentleness when she talked about him.

"Oh yes, he sure did. I loved to sing. It was probably the one thing I was better at than my big sister. In my eyes, Martha was perfect. Beautiful, sweet, funny, and had a handsome husband. But she couldn't sing worth a lick."

Rebekah laughed, fondness for her sister also glittering in her eyes.

"You should sing with me some time," Gregory said. "I could play the harpsichord."

"No. No, I can't. I don't sing anymore." Her eyes suddenly filled with deep sadness.

"Why not?"

"I'm not ready to tell you, Gregory. I might never be. Please don't ask me about it."

"Okay. I won't press you. But Rebekah, I hope you know you can trust me with anything you want to tell me."

"I do trust you," Rebekah said.

Then why won't you tell me what happened?

"You know I would never judge you for anything you might have done in your life."

"You say that now," she responded wearily.

Gregory cared deeply for her, and it was difficult for him to imagine her doing anything so terrible that she couldn't tell him about it. Besides, whatever it was, it happened more than two hundred and fifty years ago. How long was she going to despise herself?

He settled back in the bench, getting closer to her. She smiled, pleased with his nearness. Gregory wondered if she would have rested her head on his shoulder if she could. How he would have loved to run his fingers through her hair. He wondered if she would have sighed with contentment at his tender touch.

The sun was setting, and the ghost tours had started to form. Gregory watched as Harry gathered his group together in the distance. His tour tonight was beginning in front of the Bruton Parish Church, which had an old creepy graveyard surrounding it.

"Does it bother you that they have ghost tours?" Gregory asked.

"Oh, no. Not at all. It's natural to be curious about such things. We used to tell ghost stories all the time when I was growing up," Rebekah said, watching the groups with interest.

"Harry's a cool guy. When I took a ghost tour, he was the guide."

Rebekah gazed shyly at him.

"What?"

"I watched you that night when you took the tour."

"You did?" he asked, eyes wide.

"I hope you're not angry."

"No, no of course not. Why did you watch me?"

"I knew you were a little afraid of me. It must have been such a shock when I appeared to you at the shop. I was going to leave you alone after that because I didn't want to scare you. Then, when I saw you join the ghost tour, I thought you might be looking for me. Trying to find out more about me."

"I was."

"I know."

They laughed together.

"I was kind of glad to see you that night. Since I knew you were curious, I figured it might be okay to come see you again," she said.

"I'm glad you did."

"Me too."

Harry and his tour made their way up the street and toward where Gregory and Rebekah sat. Harry was telling his group about ghostly sightings at the courthouse as well as those at the local taverns. Some of the stories Gregory had heard on his tour and some were new to him.

"It's funny. Harry loves giving these ghost tours, but he's really bummed that he's never actually seen a ghost himself," he said.

"I know," she said as she watched Harry. "I hear him complain about it all the time. Never to the people in the group, though. He doesn't lie to them, but he sidesteps the question when they ask him if he's ever seen anything himself. And, of course, they ask him all the time."

Gregory eyed her curiously.

"What?" she asked.

"You could always ..."

"I could always what? Oh, you mean I could give him a real ghostly sighting."

"Yeah. Man, he would go nuts. But I know you hate doing that kind of thing."

"You do?" she asked curiously. "What makes you say that?"

"I just always get the feeling you don't like being thought of as," he glanced around, confirming there was no one within earshot. "As a ghost. You just want to be thought of as a person, which is totally understandable."

"Yes. I do feel that way." She nodded. "I don't want to be scary or ghoulish."

"You're not, you know. I never think of you that way. I just think of you as this incredibly beautiful woman who I'm lucky enough to be able to spend time with."

"Thank you," she said, that familiar look of gratitude in her eyes. She turned and watched Harry talk to his group. In fact, he was talking about *her*. "It would make him really happy, wouldn't it?"

"Yeah."

"I'll do it." Her face shone with mischief and joy.

"You can hear her weeping as she walks by," Harry was telling his group.

"That's my cue, isn't it?"

"Yep," Gregory said with a grin.

Rebekah stood up, glanced around to make sure no one was looking at her, then disappeared into thin air. It was rather fascinating. Gregory turned to watch the ghost group and waited for her dramatic appearance.

"People have seen the woman in the white dress with the pink flower design walking these very streets late at night, her long hair flowing down her back," Harry said, pausing for dramatic effect. The tour group members looked around as if expecting the Weeping Woman to show up any minute.

And then she did.

Rebekah faded into view at the back of the group, facing Harry. He drew in a sharp breath, too surprised to speak, but the tourists all turned to see what he was looking at. Shocked gasps and murmurs erupted from the group, along with mutterings of skepticism and disbelief. After all, none of the tour group members had seen her appear. They just turned to see a lady dressed like the Weeping Woman. One who managed to show up just as Harry had mentioned her.

Gregory grinned. He couldn't blame them for not believing. Rebekah stood there for a moment, looking left to right, giving all the tourists a chance to see her. She made direct eye contact with Harry, smiled at him, and then vanished.

Then came the screams.

Several of the tourists took off running, while the rest of the group stood rooted to the spot, stunned. Gregory chuckled as he watched the pandemonium. Harry punched his fist in the air in celebration, like he'd just won the Super Bowl. Though Harry had desperately wanted to have a ghost encounter, it was entirely possible he would freak out once he got one. On the contrary, the man was positively giddy, and Gregory was happy for him. Hopefully, Rebekah was still around, invisible, watching to see what happened.

"You guys saw that, right? You saw her! That was the Weeping Woman! Wow!" Harry exclaimed to the brave souls who had remained on the tour with him. "Isn't she beautiful?"

She sure is.

Sitting back on the bench, Gregory enjoyed the commotion Rebekah had caused. It suddenly occurred to him there was no way she could come back and sit with him now that she had been seen. No doubt the image of the ghostly woman with the flowered dress was burned into the memory of those who saw her. The lucky ghost-hunters who had glimpsed Rebekah were happily spreading the word to the other ghost tours. People milled around all over in search of the Weeping Woman.

Gregory stood and walked toward the place where Rebekah had appeared. She had said some people were naturally sensitive to the presence of ghosts; he wished he was one of those people, so he would know if Rebekah was still here. He concentrated for a moment but couldn't feel anything. He wanted to see her again before he went home, so he headed back to Hay's Cabinetmaker's Shop in the hopes that she would do the same.

He grinned widely when he caught sight of her standing on the bridge in the dark.

"You were a big hit," he told her.

Rebekah laughed. "Good. I'm so glad."

She did look happy, which relieved Gregory's worry that people's frightened reactions at the sight of her had upset her.

"It was really nice of you to do that. I know it meant a lot to Harry. He'll be telling the story of seeing the Weeping Woman for the rest of his life."

"Oh, I was happy to do it. Really. Being the way I am," she said, holding her hands out helplessly. "It's so rare to have the chance to help anyone anymore. It felt really good."

She had such a sweet smile, and he thought she had never looked more beautiful.

"You're a good woman, Rebekah."

She looked doubtful, but Gregory had no doubts. Whatever she had done wrong in life, she had paid her penance, and then some.

"It's getting late. You need to go home and get some rest," she said.

"I hate leaving you."

"I know. It's all right. Go. Please rest."

"You're always worrying about me."

"I am," she said, gray eyes twinkling. "And I think you like it."

"I do," he said with a grin.

Rebekah touched his lips with her fingers. The sensation was cold, and yet it still made him feel warm all over.

"Good night," she said softly and then disappeared.

13

More than a month had gone by, and Rebekah had spent nearly every day with Gregory. He even came back to the historical district on days when he wasn't working, just to see her. Rebekah marveled at how they never became bored when they were together, though they spent each day doing the same things. Sitting under a tree while Gregory ate lunch, sitting on benches and watching people. She had never been happier in her entire, long existence on Earth.

Rebekah walked past Market Square, which was quite busy this time of year. It was nearly summer, and tourists were out enjoying the sunshine and purchasing straw hats from the market to keep the sun out of their eyes.

"Hey there, pretty lady," Orlando called to her as he made long strides to catch up to her.

She stopped walking to allow him to reach her. She thrilled at being called "pretty lady" by a handsome man. It was one of those things that made her feel normal again.

"Hello, Orlando. How are you?" Rebekah asked, taking

care to keep her distance. She wanted Orlando to keep thinking of her as a woman and not a freakish dead thing.

"I see you around with my pal Gregory quite a bit lately." She smiled at the mention of Gregory's name.

"Yes, in fact I'm headed over to the cabinetmaker's shop right now to see him."

"Well," Orlando said, folding his arms and looking at her sternly. "I hope your intentions with him are honorable."

"I'm not sure I can promise that. I confess to having some rather wicked thoughts about him." Her heart raced at admitting such a risqué notion to another man. She didn't regret her words, though.

Orlando chuckled and then held out his fist for her to bump it. "Niiiice."

"Oh, hush up with you," she said, laughing and waving him off. She'd gotten rather adept at avoiding physical contact with people.

Orlando grinned. "You guys are cute together."

"Thanks."

"He's a really good guy."

"I know," Rebekah said. Orlando seemed quite pleased that Gregory had a woman in his life.

"Well, go on now. Don't keep him waiting."

"Okay. I'll see you later," she said.

"Give him a kiss from me!" Orlando called after her as she walked away.

I can't even give him a kiss from me.

Once she got to the shop, and after making sure no one was looking, she went invisible and walked through the wall to get inside. Gregory was alone, getting ready to close up.

"Hello, handsome," she said after turning visible again.

He whirled around, his eyes lighting up when he saw her. "Hey, beautiful. You're early."

She usually arrived a little past 5pm and waited for him outside on the bridge.

"I was hoping you would play for me."

"Of course," Gregory said with a grin. He finished putting his carving tools away, wiped his hands on his pants, and headed over to the harpsichord. "What would you like to hear?"

"How about 'Whistle and I'll Come to You'?"

"You got it." After shuffling his sheet music and finding the song, he began to play. Rebekah loved the fast, upbeat song. She tapped her foot in time to the music, even though she couldn't feel it and, even more annoying, it made no sound. One of the many little things she missed about being alive.

Her phantom heart raced as she watched Gregory play. His shoulders moved in time with the beat, and his fingers danced rapidly yet gracefully across the keys. His sweet brown eyes flashed with excitement as he played, and the music he made was catchy and joyous.

"Wonderful!" Rebekah proclaimed. "I wish I could applaud for you."

Gregory grinned at her, setting her heart to racing again.

"Will you play one more?" she asked. Though she could have listened to him play all night, she didn't want to delay his evening meal. Rebekah knew he had been more cautious since the day he had gotten so ill, but she couldn't take any chances.

"Anything you like."

"How about 'An American Song'?"

"That's such a pretty one. Will you sing it for me?" he ventured.

Rebekah shook her head sadly. "I'm sorry," she said in a soft voice.

"Don't be. I shouldn't have asked."

"It's all right." She wished she could. The selfish, prideful part of her wanted desperately to sing for him. He loved music, and she had a pretty voice. He would admire her for it, and it would be so flattering to hear his praise. But she would not sing for him. Not now. Not ever.

Rebekah felt terrible for spoiling the mood. "Do you sing, Gregory?"

He shrugged. "I *can* sing. I have a good ear for music, and I can sing on key, but I have a kinda plain voice that's not all that exciting to listen to."

He began to play "An American Song" for her. Once again, she watched him, his large manly hands somehow creating a tender, haunting sound. He even sang one of the verses for her. Gregory was spot on concerning his description of his voice. He hit all the notes just right, but his voice was rather ordinary. Even so, it sounded lovely to Rebekah's ears.

"Beautiful," she whispered when he finished. "Just beautiful. Thank you for playing that for me."

"Any time," he said as he gazed into her eyes. Rebekah had a sudden, delicious vision of Gregory making passionate love to her in bed as romantic music played in the background. He was always full of passion when he made music, and it was easy to imagine what he would look like as he made love to her. He would have that same look of intensity in his eyes as when he played an especially emotional song.

"We'd better get going," Rebekah said, feeling breathless despite her lack of actual breath.

Gregory stood up and gathered his things, including his dinner in a brown paper bag, and they headed out together.

Rebekah gazed up at the sky apprehensively. Some dark clouds had gathered, and there was the threat of rain in the humid air. She hated when it rained because she had to cut her time with Gregory short. He insisted he didn't mind getting wet, but she wouldn't hear of it. Going inside a crowded shop or tavern was far too risky. Someone might bump into her, causing a terrific panic. Her dates with him had to be safely inside Hay's shop, outside, or nothing.

They reached their usual spot under the tree and, so far, it wasn't raining. Gregory took out his peanut butter sandwich, a little baggie of carrots, and his unsweetened iced tea.

Rebekah shook her head sadly.

"What's wrong?"

"That's not a good dinner for you, Gregory. You deserve something so much better."

She was overcome with guilt that he wasn't at home eating a hot meal.

"Would you cook something for me if you could?" he asked.

Her eyes lit up. "Of course I would. I would make anything you wanted. What's your favorite meal?"

He thought for a moment. "I think my favorite meal would have to be spaghetti and meatballs. I gotta be careful with the pasta because I'm diabetic, but it's okay in small doses."

"And here you are with your sad, cold sandwich. I wish I could cook for you, Gregory," she said wistfully. "I wish I could cook for you and then be able to sit at the dinner table with you."

Gregory slowly put down his sandwich. She watched him carefully, worried that something was wrong.

"This," he said, more to himself than to her.

"What?" she asked cautiously.

He lifted his head and gazed directly into Rebekah's eyes. "*This*. This is what it's supposed to feel like."

"What *what's* supposed to feel like," she asked, hope swelling in her heart. She had a feeling she knew what he was saying, but it would crush her if it turned out she'd misunderstood.

"Love," he said simply. "This is what it's supposed to feel like. I love you, Rebekah."

She stared into Gregory's beautiful dark eyes. His beauty, inside and out, overwhelmed her. Overcome, she couldn't speak.

He seemed nervous, wiping his shaky hands on his pants, and she knew she had to find her voice. Find a way to express the depths of her feelings for him, lest he think she didn't feel the same way.

"Gregory," she began gently. She could see the mixture of fear and hope in his eyes. "I think I've been in love with you since the day I first laid eyes on you."

He let out a sigh of relief. How brave he had been to be the first to express his love. Her heart filled with joy to finally be able to tell him how she felt about him.

"The moment I first saw you walk into the cabinetmaker's building. Oh, you looked so strong and handsome. I couldn't take my eyes off you. I still can't," she said, her eyes unwavering from his. "And once I heard you play the harpsichord, I knew I had lost my heart forever."

Gregory's sweet eyes softened, and she could see how much her words meant to him. She understood how important music was to him. She understood everything about him. Which was why she loved him so much.

"For so long, I second-guessed myself," he said. "Like I

told you, I kept thinking maybe I was crazy for feeling like there was something wrong with my marriage. I knew I wasn't happy, and yet I thought maybe that was normal. I know better now. The way I feel when I'm with you is ... well ... it just feels right."

Rebekah nodded. She moved in closer to him, wishing with all her heart he could put his arms around her and hold her close.

"I feel like I've known you much longer than I have," she told him.

"I feel the same way." Gregory touched her lips with his fingers. She knew that was his way of saying how much he wanted to kiss her.

"I'm sorry you have the misfortune of being in love with a useless woman." She clenched her phantom fists, frustrated at her inability to touch him. She knew it was probably even worse for him. He had a physical body, and with it came physical needs.

"You're not useless, Rebekah. It's not your fault you're, you know, the way you are," Gregory said, careful not to say out loud that she was dead. There were too many people walking by for that.

"I'm just sorry that you're stuck with me instead of being with a real girlfriend who can do all the normal things with you," she said. "You're stuck hanging around your workplace all the time. We can't go anywhere or do anything—"

"I know," he said. "That's what makes it so crazy. I've done all those things before with real girlfriends. I had a real *wife*, for God's sake. And yet, I'm so much happier being with you."

"How is that possible?" she asked.

"Because just being with you is enough. Talking with

you, playing music with you, sitting with you. It makes me happier than I've been in a long, long time."

It won't always be enough.

She closed her eyes, willing those thoughts away. Gregory loved her. He'd said the words she'd been dreaming of for so long. That was what she needed to focus on now.

"Rebekah? Are you all right?" he asked.

She opened her eyes.

"What are you thinking about right now?"

"I'm thinking you'll eventually get tired of living with me like this," she said, gesturing around at the historical district where they spent all their time. She was surprised at her own confession. She'd had no intention of telling him what she was thinking, but his question had sounded so insistent.

"I won't ever get tired of you, Rebekah."

A sense of calm swept over her, and she realized why she had confessed her fears to him. She'd known he'd understand.

"I know it bothers you that we can't do all the normal things that other couples do, but I'm okay with it. I really am. As long as I'm with you, I'm happy. Because I love you."

"I love you too," she told him. "Now please eat your sandwich before you get sick."

"Yes, my love," Gregory said with a sexy grin that sent shivers of delight through her. As he finished his cold dinner, they lapsed into their familiar comfortable silence. The crowds began to thin as it got later in the evening.

"It doesn't make sense," he said at last. "That we should meet now, when there's no way we can possibly be together."

Rebekah saw the sadness in his eyes. It was as if she'd had a fatal disease or something. She and Gregory were together and in love, but there was no telling for how long.

All they knew was it couldn't last. There was an expiration date. Their love story was already over before it had begun.

"I don't know. Sometimes I think maybe we were meant to meet so I could help you. Help you get where you're supposed to go," he said.

"Being with you doesn't give me much motivation to cross over. I don't want to leave you."

"I know. But eventually ..."

"I don't want to talk about that," she said, shaking her head.

"Okay. We don't have to talk about it now. I meant it when I said I'm happy just being with you."

"Me too," she said, sitting as close to him as possible and gazing into his eyes.

Gregory looked down and smiled adoringly at her.

Then it began to rain.

14

It rained all the next day and Ben was working at the shop, so Rebekah was unable to visit with Gregory. Once again, she was frustrated at the many limitations of being dead. Her deepest fear was that he would meet someone new. Someone who could actually go out on dates with him in the evenings. A woman who could eat and drink with him. Who could hold him, touch him. Kiss him. She would probably even sing for him.

Rebekah scolded herself for refusing to sing for Gregory. There were so many things she couldn't do for him, and the one thing he'd asked of her, she'd refused.

Still, she had her reasons for never singing again, and she knew she wouldn't change her mind. It would serve her right if Gregory grew bored with her and deserted her.

Finally, on Saturday, the rain cleared up. He had the day off, but he'd promised to come back to the historical district to spend the day with her. She waited for him under their usual tree across the street from the busy Market Square. The weather was gorgeous. The thick crowds of people meant that Rebekah had to be careful while walking the streets during the daytime. Before meeting Gregory, she had spent little time among the living. Now she was around people all the time.

Sitting under the tree, watching the breeze blow through the trees and wallowing in her usual self-loathing, she spotted him walking toward her. His face lit up when he saw her, and her heart soared. Often, she'd be feeling bad about herself, obsessing over all the mistakes she had made in her life, and then Gregory would look at her like she was a person of worth. His presence gave her a sense of peace; he made her feel like she was worth loving.

He loves me because he doesn't know what I did.

No. She would not think of that today. Today, she would allow herself to be happy and bask in his love.

Rebekah stood up to greet him.

"Hello, Gregory. Have you—"

"Yes, I've eaten," he said with a smile. She knew by now he always took good care of himself, and she didn't need to check on him. Even so, she couldn't help worrying.

"It's good to see you," Gregory said, touching her lips with his fingers. "I've been going crazy without you."

"Me too. Do you want to sit, or do you want to walk?"

"Let's walk," he said.

They fell into step together with Rebekah walking on the inside toward the buildings and Gregory walking closer to the street. It was safer that way, with him shielding her from the tourists walking around.

"I talked to my parents last night. I usually call them once a week. It's strange not to tell them about you. You're the most important person in my life, and they don't even know you exist."

Though it saddened her to know he couldn't tell his

family about her, her sorrow was far overshadowed by the thrill of being called the most important person in his life.

"I considered telling them about you. That I'm seeing someone. But then, of course, they would want to meet you."

Rebekah nodded, imagining how it would feel to be introduced to Gregory's family as his girlfriend.

"I would have loved to meet them," she said.

"And they'd have been crazy about you."

"Do you think so?" Rebekah asked, wrinkling her nose.

"Of course they would."

"They might believe me to be a homewrecker that broke up your marriage. Or at the very least, they'd probably wonder why you're with me and not Vanessa."

"That occurred to me too. What they would think the first time I brought a new woman home. My parents are nice people, not the judgmental type at all. Even so, I wouldn't blame them for scrutinizing my new girlfriend."

"Nor would I."

"But it would be amazing if I were able to bring you home with me. I've never really been able to explain why my marriage broke up. My family loved Vanessa, and with good reason. I think if I brought you home, they'd take one look at us together and they would finally get it, you know?"

"You have thought a lot about this, haven't you?"

He chuckled. "Yeah, I guess I have."

They made their way down Duke of Gloucester Street and turned to walk on the Palace Green. It was safer on the grass and away from the crowds on the streets.

"You look handsome today."

Gregory glanced down at his attire: blue jeans and a gray T-shirt with a logo from a Florida bar and restaurant on it.

"Thanks. Just something I threw on this morning. I was in a hurry to come see you. You, however, look beautiful."

"I look the same as I always do," Rebekah said. She couldn't even wear makeup for him, and she felt so ordinary compared to the pretty women she saw all around her. Even when they wore shorts and T-shirts, the tourist women often wore jewelry and makeup, and some had their nails done.

"Yeah. Like I said, you look beautiful."

Rebekah *felt* beautiful when he complimented her. Just a moment ago she had thought herself plain and boring, but Gregory's sweet words made her feel feminine and attractive. She looked around at all the trees, bursting with blossoms, and up at the gorgeous blue sky. If she were alive, she would have taken a deep, cleansing breath of fresh air.

Then Gregory did just that; he inhaled deeply and let out his breath. It made her smile to know they were so in sync that way.

As the two got closer to the Governor's Palace, Rebekah's eyes grew wide.

"Oh, Gregory! Look!"

He turned to see what she was so excited about, then chuckled.

A wedding was taking place on the lawn of the palace. The bride's ornate, flowing gown gleamed in the sunlight.

"It's so lovely," Rebekah gushed.

"Come on. Let's go get a closer look." He clearly enjoyed her enthusiasm.

They neared the festivities, while keeping a respectful distance. The bride was a lovely Hispanic woman, with her dark hair styled in curly ringlets that cascaded down her back.

"Oh, she's just beautiful, isn't she?" Rebekah said.

Gregory nodded.

"And he looks incredibly handsome," she said, admiring the groom in his tuxedo. "They look so joyful, don't they?"

"Yes, they certainly do," Gregory said. "Couldn't have asked for a better day for an outdoor wedding."

Rebekah's heart filled with elation as she watched the happy couple gaze into each other's eyes. The ceremony must just have ended, and they were greeting their family and friends amid laughter and some tears. Rebekah said a quick prayer to God, asking Him to grant the newlyweds a long and happy life together.

"It's so *romantic*," Rebekah gushed, making Gregory chuckle. She loved that little laugh of his. He wasn't laughing at her—he'd meant it when he'd said he thought her girlieness was cute. She turned to him and said, "'The sight of lovers feedeth those in love.'"

Gregory smiled. "*As You Like It*."

She laughed, thrilled that he never failed to recognize her Shakespeare quotes. He pressed his fingers to her lips. She loved that sweet gesture. Doing it now showed her that seeing the wedding had affected him a little, too. They looked into each other's eyes, allowing her a delicious moment to imagine what his lips would feel like on hers.

Finally tearing her gaze away, she smiled at the newly married couple. The groom had his arm around his new bride in a warm and loving embrace. From their sweet, intimate body language, Rebekah had high hopes that this would be a happy marriage.

"They have their whole lives ahead of them," she said wistfully. Almost without thinking, she blurted out," Would you marry me, Gregory? If you could?"

"Are you proposing?" he asked, a twinkle of amusement in his eye.

She laughed, deciding she might as well go for it. "Yes, I guess I am."

"I would marry you in a heartbeat if I could."

"You mean you'd marry me if I *had* a heartbeat."

Gregory laughed. "Yes. Yes, I sure would. And I wouldn't even be afraid."

She looked at him quizzically. "What do you mean?" He hadn't seemed afraid of her since their initial meeting. All her past worries about him thinking she was gross and disgusting because she was dead suddenly came flooding back.

"I've been really scared about the idea of getting married again."

"Oh," she said, relief coursing through her.

"But I didn't even have to think when you asked me just now. It's just *yes*. Easily a yes. I've always wanted to get married again, but I was terrified of making another mistake. I wouldn't ever want to go through a divorce again, and I can't stand the idea of putting another woman through that again either. But with you, I don't have any of those worries. And it's not because it's not possible for us to get married. It's because I have no doubts about us. That we would be happy."

"Wow," she said softly.

"Mrs. Rebekah Markham."

"Oh, can you imagine?" she cried, putting her hand near her heart. "That sounds so perfect, doesn't it? Rebekah Markham." It wasn't the first time she had fantasized about taking his name.

"Yes, it does sound perfect. I would give anything to marry you, Rebekah. I would marry you, and then on our wedding night, I would make love to you all night long."

Normally calm and reserved, his eyes filled with hunger.

He *wanted* her. He wanted to take her to his bed and claim her as his own. And she wanted to let him.

"That would be so wonderful, Gregory," she said. "You would have been worth waiting two hundred and fifty years for."

A ripple of scandalous excitement went through Rebekah as she realized they were both fantasizing about what they would do on their wedding night.

Standing on the palace lawn with the strains of a string quartet softly playing nearby, they gazed into each other's eyes.

"Do you want to dance?" Gregory asked.

"What? We can't dance. It's not possible."

"Sure it is," he said with a grin. He held up his hand in position, as if ready to grasp her hand and lead her in a dance. "Come on!"

Rebekah giggled and put her hand up to nearly touch his. They began to move in rhythm to the music. From a distance, it was probably impossible to tell that they weren't actually touching.

"This is wonderful, Gregory," she said dreamily. She had always dreamed of dancing on the arm of a handsome suitor. Until now, she didn't think she had any dreams left that could possibly come true. Leave it to sweet Gregory to figure out a way.

As she danced with the love of her life on the luscious green palace lawn, Rebekah allowed the delicious truth of his words to sink in. He had said he would marry her if he could. Something in the way he looked at her made her feel like perhaps she wasn't a completely terrible person. If someone as dear as Gregory could love her, maybe there was some hope for her soul after all.

15

Gregory was heading toward Hay's Cabinetmaker's Shop to start his shift Friday morning when he heard a commotion. The commotion turned out to be laughter, as Orlando was in the middle of performing a fiery speech in front of the courthouse. He was yelling something about treason. Gregory didn't know where the guy got that kind of energy so early in the morning. Quite a crowd had gathered, and they seemed highly entertained by his antics. Gregory laughed and shook his head as he walked past.

"You there!" Orlando boomed in his stage voice.

Gregory closed his eyes and let out a breath. He opened his eyes, turned, and shot Orlando a warning look. He knew Gregory had no desire to be dragged into his public act.

"You would make a fine soldier. Look at the strapping, handsome man, folks!" Orlando said, pointing his finger and drawing everyone's attention to Gregory.

He felt his face get hot. Though Orlando would never do anything to make any of the guests at Williamsburg feel uncomfortable, friends were fair game to him.

"I must go over and speak to this young man and recruit him," Orlando said, addressing the crowd. "And now, I want each and every one of you to go out and spread the word. Recruit more soldiers!" No one moved. "Go on. Off with you!"

People laughed, finally getting the hint that his presentation was over. They went off on their separate ways. Grinning, Orlando strode over to Gregory.

"Man, why you gotta do that to me?"

"Because it's funny," Orlando said with an evil cackle. "And because you're such an easy target. I know how much you hate the attention. And actually, this time I singled you out because I did want to talk to you."

"Yeah? Why?"

"I go to Amber Ox pretty much every Friday night after work. Sometimes I meet my buddies there, and sometimes it's just me up at the bar. So I wanted to ask if you wanted to go tonight."

"Aw, man, I can't tonight." Gregory had plans to be with Rebekah. He spent most evenings with her, except for those times when she insisted that he take a break from being at his workplace and go home.

"Okay, well it's a regular thing. Like I said, pretty much every Friday night. It's a standing offer."

"Great. Thanks."

"Sure thing."

Gregory glanced over at the courthouse building where Orlando had been performing.

"Think I'll go around the back way to work from now on," he said.

Orlando cackled and clapped him on the back.

∼

AFTER WORK, Gregory found Rebekah waiting out on the bridge as usual.

"Gregory," she began, her tone somewhat serious.

"Everything okay?" he asked.

"Oh, yes. I'm just fine. Gregory," she said firmly, "I want you to go out with Orlando tonight."

"What?"

"I overheard him ask you this morning about going out with him."

"You did? Where were you?"

"Watching Orlando perform," she said. "I was nearby, just invisible. I saw him picking on you. You're so cute when you blush."

He chuckled, slightly uncomfortable that Rebekah had witnessed that spectacle.

"Darling, I love you so much and I love being with you every moment I can, but you need other people in your life. *Living* people. I want you to go and have a drink with him. It will be good for you."

"But I'd much rather be with you," Gregory insisted.

Rebekah smiled. "I can't tell you how much I love hearing you say that. But it's important to me that you have other friends in your life and that you have a chance to go other places, instead of being stuck here all the time."

Gregory opened his mouth to argue, but she wouldn't allow it.

"I want you to go. I love you. I'll see you tomorrow, darling," Rebekah said. She pressed her fingers to his lips, and then she disappeared.

He sighed, knowing there was nothing he could do to make her stay with him tonight.

As he headed toward the bus stop at the Visitor Center parking lot, he was surprised to find himself looking forward to going out. He'd meant it when he'd said he would much rather be with Rebekah, but he had to admit it would be nice to get out for a while. For the last several months, he had spent the vast majority of his time in the Williamsburg historical district, either working or hanging out with Rebekah.

Gregory found Orlando sitting at the bar at Amber Ox Brewery and Restaurant with empty seats on both sides of him. The rest of the barstools were occupied. Clearly, none of Orlando's other friends had shown up tonight. At least not yet.

"Hey there," Gregory said as he sat down on the stool to Orlando's left. The place had a friendly vibe to it. The type of joint where regulars hung out, but tourists could also feel comfortable bringing their kids for dinner.

"You made it," he said with a grin. "Good to see ya. Hey, Leo, put his tab on mine."

"No, don't—"

"I got it, man. First time you hang out here, it's on me. Next time, you're on your own."

"Fair enough. Thanks, man. Believe me, my tab won't be too high."

"Not much of a drinker, huh?" Orlando asked as he raised his own mug of beer to his lips.

"Couldn't be if I wanted to," Gregory said to Orlando, and then he told the bartender, "The Belgian lager. Thanks! Being diabetic, beer's not great for me. But one won't hurt."

"Cool."

Gregory looked around the restaurant. It was a small place, the type of bar where locals would hang out. They had signs advertising a Mug Club, which Orlando was clearly a part of since he had a mug with the number 189 on it.

The bartender set down his beer, and Gregory nodded his thanks.

"Oh, man. This is great," he said, sipping his beer. He didn't drink a lot, but he knew a high-quality microbrew when he tasted one.

"They got the best stuff here."

"This is a cool place. I've never been here before," Gregory said.

"That's because you never leave work."

"What?"

"Seriously, dude. You're there, like, all the time. Every time I gotta stay late for a meeting or to catch up on stuff, you're there with that girl of yours." Orlando looked at him a tad suspiciously.

"What?" Gregory repeated.

"Nothing. It's none of my business."

"What's none of your business? What are you talking about?"

"Well, it's just you said Rebekah's unavailable, right?"

"You could say that, I guess."

"And you guys are together all the time at the historical district. You never seem to go anywhere else. Tell me the truth. Is she married?"

"Oh," Gregory said with a laugh. "No. No, of course not. I would never be with a married woman. But I get why you would think that."

He suddenly wondered if anybody else had been thinking that, though he couldn't think of anyone who might be paying that much attention to his comings and goings. Ben maybe, but he worked only part time and wasn't around that much.

"She seems to be really into you."

"Yeah."

"And I *know* you're into her," Orlando said, looking understandably confused. After all, if Rebekah wasn't married, it was hard to explain why they weren't together.

"Yeah," Gregory said again.

Orlando waited for an explanation. When he realized none was forthcoming, he changed the subject.

"You want something to eat?" he asked. "They got good bar food here. Mostly appetizers. Nothing fancy, but it's pretty good."

"Yeah, sure," Gregory said, already feeling light-headed from the beer. He smiled to himself, thinking how Rebekah would scold him for not eating yet if she were here now.

Orlando slid the menu over to him, and they decided to split some chicken wings and french fries. The food arrived fairly quickly, and as they ate, they talked about work and how things would start getting busier now that it was after Memorial Day and the summer crowds would begin to arrive. Eventually, the conversation shifted to the women Orlando was dating.

"I haven't really been out on that many dates lately," he said.

"Is that so?" Gregory asked. "Everybody says you're quite the ladies' man."

Orlando laughed. "I guess you could say that. I have my fun."

"I guess you can do that when you're, you know."

"I'm what?"

"You're ..." Gregory gestured at Orlando.

"Ruggedly handsome?" he suggested.

Gregory laughed. "Yes. Let's call it that. Rebekah thinks you're quite handsome. She told me so."

Orlando eyed him curiously.

"*What* already?"

"Nothing. Like I said before, it's none of my business. Look, you don't have to tell me a thing if you don't want to, but I've seen the way you look at that girl."

After hesitating briefly, Gregory admitted, "I love her."

"I had a feeling."

"But there can't ever be anything between us."

"Why the hell not? Unless I'm crazy, she looks at you the same way."

"Yeah. She does. She loves me too."

Orlando held out his hands in confusion.

"It's hard to explain," Gregory said. "Suffice it to say, I would literally have to move Heaven and Earth to be with her."

Without a trace of his usual goofiness, Orlando stared sternly at Gregory and said, "Then do it."

"I can't."

Orlando let out a frustrated sigh. It was kind of nice that he cared enough about his happiness to be annoyed by his apparent lack of action.

Gregory fiddled with the paper coaster on the bar. "I'm debating about how much I should tell you."

"It might help to talk about it. Just sayin'."

Gregory reflected on the day he'd spilled his guts to Orlando about his divorce. Orlando was a jokester to be sure, but when it came down to it, he was a loyal friend. Gregory had felt better after talking to him about Vanessa, and he never felt judged. The burden of keeping Rebekah's story a secret from everyone he knew was heavy. He couldn't tell his family about her. Until now, there was nobody he felt he could confide in.

He glanced around at all the people sitting close by. "Not here."

"How 'bout we move over to one of those tables in the

back?" Orlando said, gesturing at an area away from the crowded bar.

"Perfect."

"Let's grab a few more beers before we move."

"Ah, I don't know."

"Come on, man. One more won't kill you." Orlando frowned. "I mean, it won't, right?"

He chuckled. "No, it won't. One more is fine."

After getting their beers and letting the bartender know they were moving to the back, Gregory's confidence wavered. Nervously, he crumpled up a paper napkin. How on earth was he going to explain this?

"Don't overthink it, dude. Just spill it," Orlando said.

Gregory laughed. That was the same advice he and Rebekah were always giving each other. No judgment, no overthinking, just say what's on your mind.

"There's some reason why you think the two of you can't be together. Just tell me what it is."

He sighed, figuring it was best to just tell the truth. "She's dead."

Orlando's eyes flew open wide. "What? My God, what happened?"

"N—no. No! Sorry. I didn't think about the way that would sound."

Naturally, Orlando looked at him as if he had completely lost his mind.

"She's not completely dead, exactly," Gregory said, knowing he was doing a terrible job at explaining the situation.

"Oh," Orlando said softly, his face growing serious. "Is she terminally ill or something?"

"Not exactly. Okay, look. You're not gonna believe what I'm gonna tell you, so I'll just say it straight out. Rebekah is still around, but she's dead. She exists only in spirit form. She's a ghost."

Gregory's tense muscles relaxed, relief coursing through him now that he had finally gotten the truth out. He watched as Orlando processed his words.

Orlando stared at him for a long moment then glanced at Gregory's half-empty beer glass.

"I'm not drunk," he said with a weary chuckle. "I know this all sounds insane, and I don't blame you one bit for not believing me, but it's the truth." He lowered his voice. "Rebekah is dead. That's not a costume she's wearing. Those are her real clothes. She died in 1762. You've heard of all the ghost stories about Williamsburg, right?"

Orlando nodded uncertainly, looking uncomfortable. He was probably wishing some of his "normal" buddies had shown up tonight, as opposed to this whack job talking about ghosts.

"You've heard of the Weeping Woman?"

Orlando nodded again.

"That's her. That's Rebekah."

"I see," he said, eying Gregory warily.

"I know, I know. It's crazy, but it's easy enough to prove. Next time you see her, try to touch her. You won't be able to. Seriously. Your hand will go right through her, and all you'll feel is a cold sensation."

"Gonna level with you, dude. My first inclination is to say you're nuts."

"Fair enough," Gregory said with a laugh. He took a sip of beer while he waited for his friend to continue.

"That being said, I admit I'm pretty sure I've had a few ghostly encounters myself," Orlando said. "I've been touched a few times near the Peyton Randolph House. I've felt something grab my ankle, and when I turn around, there's nothing there. People say one of the slaves haunts that house."

He appeared more interested than scared about the idea of ghosts.

"That's Jackey. Rebekah knows her. At least, she knows of her."

"Oh," Orlando said. He didn't seem to know what to make of that statement. "Well, I don't think Jackey likes me very much."

"I don't think she's too fond of white people."

Orlando smiled sadly. "I guess not. Can't exactly blame her. She grabbed me pretty hard one night. I told myself it was my imagination. But then I saw the bruise later that night."

"Wow."

"Yeah. So I guess you could say I do believe in ghosts. It's funny. I was talking to one of the guys who runs the ghost tours. He swore to me he actually saw the Weeping Woman during one of his tours."

"Yes, yes he did! I was there. Rebekah hates being thought of as dead. She doesn't want anybody to know, but when she realized how badly Harry wanted a ghost encounter, she let him see her."

"Hmm," Orlando said.

"I know you probably think I'm out of my mind. That's why it took me so long to tell you. Sometimes I have a hard time believing it myself. And yet, when I'm with her, I don't think of her as being, you know, that way. To me, she's just Rebekah Jennings."

"The woman you love," Orlando said simply. He still looked uncertain, but not as much as he had a moment ago. He'd known Gregory long enough to know he was a pretty stable person who didn't generally go around making up wild stories.

"Yes."

"Jennings," Orlando said thoughtfully.

"Yeah, like the tavern. Her family owned the Jennings Tavern."

"Wow," Orlando said. He took a healthy gulp of his beer as he mulled things over.

"So that's why you see me around the historic district all the time. She's limited in how far she can go. Seems to be just a few miles from where she lived and died."

"How did she die?" Orlando asked.

"She drowned."

"Oh, that's right. I forgot."

"Yeah. That's about all I know. She doesn't like to talk about what happened to her. I wish she would, though. I mean, she can't stay trapped here forever."

"What do you mean?"

"She's been living—well, *existing*—this way for over two hundred and fifty years. She can see and hear, and she's retained her mind and her soul, but she can't smell or taste or touch anything. Ever since she died, she's been stuck." Gregory sighed heavily. "There's no hope I could ever be with her, so the only thing I can do is help set her free. Help her to heal from whatever happened so she can cross over and finally be at peace."

It felt particularly awful to say the words out loud. Between the alcohol and spilling his guts, he felt dangerously close to tears. That was the last thing he needed. To have an emotional breakdown in the middle of a crowded bar.

"I—I guess I'd better get going," he said, hearing his own

anguish in his voice. "Thanks for the beer and the food. I promise I'll get the tab next time."

Orlando looked concerned as he watched Gregory get up from the table.

"Thanks for listening. Like I said, I know it's nuts, but I'm telling you the truth. You can find out for yourself the next time you see Rebekah. Just try to touch her. I mean, ask her first. It upsets her to be thought of as dead."

"I would never think that about her," Orlando said. He was clearly still unsure about the whole situation, but Gregory appreciated the compassion in his voice.

"More than anything, she just wants to be thought of as a person. A woman. Just, next time you see her, try to touch her. You won't be able to," Gregory said sadly. "Believe me. I've tried."

16

Feeling emotionally drained, Gregory collapsed into bed as soon as he got home. It had helped to confide in his friend, even if that friend wasn't sure what to believe. Orlando would figure out soon enough that he was telling the truth about Rebekah, and it was nice to have someone to share this highly unique predicament with.

Even so, Gregory somehow felt worse about the situation. Saying the words out loud had really hit him hard.

There's no hope that I could ever be with her, so the only thing I can do is help set her free.

Getting lost in euphoria was easy when he was with Rebekah. There were moments when he would forget that she was no longer alive. Laughing and talking with her always felt so natural. So right. Time flew by when they were together, and it was only at the end of the evening, when he had to leave her alone in the dark, that reality came crashing down on him.

Gregory could no longer afford to ignore the reality. When it came right down to it, he was prolonging the inevitable. He had meant it when he'd said he would marry her if he could. Those cursed wedding vows taunted him now.

Until death do us part.

Gregory and Rebekah were already separated by death, and it was only a matter of time until they were separated forever. The pain of that reality crushed him.

He closed his eyes, finally allowing the tears to fall. As devastating as it was, he knew he would have to let go of the woman he loved more than life itself.

Rebekah was suffering. She had already suffered for far too long, and it was time he helped put an end to it.

He'd said all along that he wanted to help Rebekah cross over and be at peace, but he had done very little to make it happen. Selfishly, he didn't want Rebekah to leave him. Whenever she said she didn't want to talk about her past, he had let the matter drop. He'd told himself it was because he didn't want to upset her. That was partly true, of course. But deep down, he knew the real reason he never pressed her was that if she finally made peace with her demons, her spirit would be set free. And he would be left behind.

Gregory knew the adage was true: if you truly loved something, you had to set it free.

The time had come to prove how much he truly loved Rebekah.

It was time to let her go.

~

GREGORY'S HEART yearned at the sight of Rebekah waiting for him on the bridge, looking lovely as always. He had missed her terribly after only one night away from her. He couldn't imagine what it would feel like to spend the rest of his life without her. But he had to be strong for her sake. Her peace and happiness were far more important than his own.

"Hi, beautiful," he said.

Rebekah smiled, making his heart jump once more.

"Hello, handsome."

"I forgot to pack a sandwich for dinner."

Her eyes opened wide. "Oh no," she said.

"It's all right. I can order something from the Christiana Campbell Tavern, and we can still sit together outside while I eat."

"Oh, good," Rebekah said, looking relieved.

They walked together down Duke of Gloucester Street, which was still crowded with the day's tourists.

"I hope you won't get mad at me, but ..." he started tentatively.

"I could never get mad at you, Gregory."

Something about that simple statement made him quite sad. They were still in somewhat of a honeymoon stage in their relationship, newly in love and not much to argue about yet. Though this attraction phase was wonderful and exciting, he found himself mourning for the long-term relationship he wanted with her. The one he would never have. The one where they got married and lived together through thick and thin. Sickness and health. Good times and bad. Silly arguments and make-up sex. All the things, big and little, that made up a lifetime.

"I told someone about you," Gregory said. "I mean, everything about you. How you're ..." He gestured at her ghostly body, unable to say the words out loud with so many people milling about.

"You did?" she asked. "Who?"

"Orlando."

Her face fell. "Oh."

"I'm sorry. I should have asked your permission first."

"It's okay," she said wearily. She didn't sound like it was okay.

"Are you mad?"

Rebekah laughed. "I'm not thrilled. But it's hard to be angry with you, Gregory."

There was such love in her eyes. No one had ever looked at him with such tenderness and admiration before. Once again, he was reminded of what had been missing from his marriage. Rebekah loved him, but she was a bit irritated with him right now. She didn't have to say it. He could tell.

"I'm sorry," he repeated.

"It's all right," she said, the weariness and irritation still in her voice. "I understand. God knows you must need *someone* to talk about all this with."

"Are you mad that it was Orlando that I told?"

He took her momentary silence as a bad sign.

"Yes," she said eventually.

"Oh."

"Oh, it's my own vanity, Gregory. Please don't feel bad about it. I guess I just hate the idea of a handsome man like Orlando knowing I'm creepy and dead."

Rebekah glanced around to make sure no one had heard what she had said, but nobody was paying them any attention.

Gregory couldn't help grimacing as a familiar surge of jealousy swirled inside him. "But it's okay that I know about you?" It was stupid, he knew. But Orlando was far better looking than him, and Rebekah found him attractive.

"In case you have forgotten, my darling, it took a matter of life and death for me to appear to you as a spirit. Of course I didn't want you to know the truth about me. I loved watching you work and listening to you play such beautiful music, and I wanted more than anything to have a chance to speak with you. I was torn up about it. I knew I could have acted like I was a worker here and spoken to you, but it was too much of a risk. I couldn't bring myself to do it."

Rebekah gazed at him lovingly, and he felt his envy subside.

"When your life was in danger, I had no choice but to let you see me. Believe me, Gregory. It broke my heart when you were afraid of me. I'll never forget the way you looked at me that day."

Her pretty face darkened with sorrow at the memory.

"I guess I never thought of it that way. I'm sorry."

"It's all right. You look at me differently now."

Gregory smiled at her. He could only hope he made her feel as good as he felt when she gazed at him.

When they arrived at the tavern, he said, "I'll run in and grab something to go. Shouldn't take too long. Unless you want to come in with me?"

Rebekah surveyed the crowd waiting on the porch of the tavern for a table. She shook her head.

"No, I'd better not. I'll wait for you on the Capitol lawn."

"Okay."

The Christina Campbell Tavern was located right across the street from the Capitol building. Gregory hadn't realized how hungry he was until he smelled the delicious food. He had planned to order a sandwich because it wouldn't take as long to make. Then his hunger won out. Realizing that not counting last night's chicken wings, it had been a while since he'd had a hot meal for dinner, he wound up ordering the tavern's corn chowder and southern fried chicken.

He found Rebekah waiting under a tree near the Capitol. Sitting down beside her, he watched her face as he unpacked his food from the large paper bag.

"Oh, that looks delicious! I'm so glad you're having a hot meal for once."

Gregory grinned. "I knew you would say that. Still feels weird to be eating like this in front of you."

"Don't feel bad about it. I can't smell it, and I'm certainly not hungry. I'm just glad to see you're being taken care of, even if I'm not the one doing it."

Grief tugged at his heart. He knew they were both mourning the loss of what might have been. The comfort of a happily married life. The ability to sit down and share a meal that Rebekah had so lovingly prepared for both of them.

Gregory needed to talk to Rebekah about so many things tonight, but he needed to take the edge off his hunger first.

"That is *so* good," he said as he devoured the tasty corn chowder. "I forgot how great their food is."

Rebekah watched happily as he finished off the soup in no time and then started on the southern fried chicken.

"So, I guess you had a good time with Orlando last night?" she asked dryly.

He laughed. "Yeah, I guess you could say that. Are you sorry you made me go?"

"No, no. Not at all." Her minor annoyance seemed to have mostly faded away already. "I am glad you had someone to talk to. What did he say when you told him?"

"Not much, really. I'm not sure he believes me. I'm pretty sure he thinks I'm nuts. Can't say I blame him. Still, it helped to talk to him, you know?"

"I'm glad," Rebekah said sincerely.

"I know he's usually such a goofy guy, but when you get

right down to it, he's a good friend. The kinda guy you end up spilling your guts to, for some reason. A while back, we were just sitting around and talking, and I ended up telling him all about my divorce. I didn't mean to. Just kinda happened. But I wasn't sorry, you know? Made me feel better."

"That's good." She smiled. "The last thing I want to do is keep you isolated."

"Yeah," Gregory said, feeling the weight of the world on his shoulders. He knew what he had to do. It was the right thing to do, but it wouldn't be easy.

"What's wrong?" she asked, her sweet gray eyes suddenly alarmed. She knew him so well. She could tell instantly when he was upset.

"We can't go on like this."

"What do you mean?" she asked. Gregory could see the fear in her eyes. "Oh. You must be so tired of coming here all the time to be with me."

"No, no, no. That's not it at all, Rebekah. It's the opposite, actually. I'm never happier than when I'm with you. You know I love you. I love you so very much, but we both know there's no possible way we can be together. Sooner or later …"

Rebekah closed her eyes and lowered her head. She knew what he was saying was true, but she didn't want to face it any more than he did. Gregory waited for her to open her eyes again before he spoke.

"I've just come to realize that the only way I can help you is to let you go." His voice cracked as he finished his sentence.

"What do you mean let me go?" He heard the panic in her voice.

"Beautiful, I won't ever leave you. I love being with you,

and I want to spend as much time as possible with you while I still can."

Rebekah nodded, listening intently to each word.

"What I mean is I need to help you cross over to Heaven. That's where you belong. You have to go sooner or later. Whether it's now or years from now, it's going to happen, and I see no reason for you to suffer any longer. God, I can't bear leaving you in the darkness every night. I would give everything I have if I could just bring you home with me, but I can't. The only thing I can do is help set you free."

"What will happen to you if I do cross over?"

"I'll grieve for you for the rest of my life," he said simply.

"Oh, Gregory," she said, putting her hand over her heart. "I don't want that for you. I want you to be happy."

"And I want *you* to be happy and at peace. And I'm not going to stop until you make it to Heaven where you belong." He reached over and touched her lips with his fingers. Even the cold touch was better than nothing. "Someday we'll be together again. Just not in this lifetime."

Her expression crumbled.

"It's all right, Rebekah. Together, we're going to make this happen. You're going to be at peace."

She looked into his eyes, hesitated a moment, then she nodded. It was such a simple gesture, but it gave Gregory hope that he might be able to help her.

"I'll try," she said. "But only because I want to set you free, too. After I'm gone, you'll be free to move on. To meet someone else."

"Rebekah—"

"I don't want to talk about it too much. I just ... I—I can't." Her eyes were filled with anguish. "It's difficult for me to think about, darling. But I really do want you to meet someone else. I want you to be married and happy and to have the children and the family you deserve."

"Rebekah, I—"

She put a hand up to silence him and shook her head. He understood. Her emotions were raw. Rebekah was, by nature, an unselfish woman. She wanted what was best for him, but that didn't mean it wasn't painful for her.

Gregory finished his dinner in silence, giving her a few minutes to collect herself. As much as he despised seeing her so upset, he knew this was going to get much worse before it got better.

"If I'm going to help you, Rebekah," he said at last, "you're going to have to tell me what happened in your life. What's keeping you here."

She nodded wearily.

"I know. I know I have to tell you. I just ..." She covered her face with her hands and wailed, "I just don't want you to hate me!"

She began to cry a tearless sob, and Gregory could hardly bear it.

"Sweetheart, it's okay. It's all right. I could never, ever hate you."

He also knew Rebekah was truly terrified he might stop loving her. All he could do was be gentle and compassionate, to help her through this.

"Okay," she whispered. "I'll tell you. But not here."

"Fine," he said. It was a bit crowded and they definitely needed privacy for this conversation. "I know just the spot."

17

The bridge behind Hay's Cabinetmaker's Shop was the perfect place to hide away and speak in private. By this time in the evening, everything on this street was closed. There were a few private residences located nearby, but there was no reason for any tourists to come walking down this particular street after hours.

Poor, sweet Rebekah was terrified. She could barely look at him. Gregory wished he could do something to ease her fears. Make her understand he would always love her, no matter what she had to say. Painful as this would be for her, he hoped with all his heart she would feel better, unburdened, once she got through it.

They had walked in near silence until they reached the back of the shop.

"Here, why don't we sit down on the grass next to the stream," Gregory suggested.

"Of course. Wherever you're most comfortable," she said. After all, it didn't matter where she sat, since she didn't feel anything. He figured the soft grass would be more comfortable than sitting or standing on the hard wooden bridge. He would stay with her all night if that was what she needed.

They got settled on the grass near the small trickling stream. The sun would set soon, and then they'd see their way by the few streetlights.

"Dear God, I don't even know where to begin," Rebekah said in a shaky voice.

Gregory cursed his inability to hold her in his arms. How he wished he could comfort her and stroke her hair lovingly. Anything to make this process easier for her.

"I know this is hard," he said. "Let's get right down to it, all right? The sooner you can get the words out about what happened, hopefully you'll feel better."

"Or you'll find out what a terrible person I am, and you'll never speak to me again."

"I swear to you, Rebekah, that *will not happen*. I will always, *always* love you. Do you understand?"

She nodded uncertainly. She didn't really believe it, but that was okay. He would do whatever it took to reassure her once this was all over.

"Okay," he began gently. "So, Rebekah, you do know why you're still stuck here on Earth after all this time."

"Yes," she said. Her eyes filled with terror. The urge to take her in his arms grew ever stronger.

"Tell me what happened, my love."

Rebekah closed her eyes, and Gregory watched as she gathered her strength.

"My little brother, Nathaniel, loved to take trips with me," she said. Her voice sounded stronger than he had expected. Rebekah had talked about her little brother many times, and it was clear how much she had loved the little guy. "He was so adorable. He was so curious, so talkative. He could wear you out sometimes! And we had this special sign between the two of us. I would put my hand over my heart," with that, she made the gesture," and he would know I was saying 'I love you' to him. I'll never forget the day he did the same thing for me. Oh, I nearly cried. It was so beautiful."

Gregory listened as she spoke fondly of her baby brother.

"Such a funny little man. He loved when I sang, especially the songs I made up just for him."

"You were a wonderful big sister."

Rebekah's smile faded.

"Yes, well. So I promised to take him to the James River one day. He loved the water. Like a little fish, he was."

Gregory smiled encouragingly.

"For a week, that was all he could talk about! He was only three years old. Little ones get so excited about such things, you know?"

He nodded.

"The trip to the river was about eight miles, so we went on horseback. I was supposed to wake him up early that morning, but I didn't have to. He bounced into my bed before dawn, up and ready to go!" Rebekah smiled wistfully at the memory. "We packed a picnic lunch so we could spend the day. It was going to be such a special day, just the two of us."

She faltered as she spoke. Looking down at the ground, she struggled to continue. Gregory's stomach filled with dread. His heart ached knowing she was in pain, and he knew something horrible had happened that day.

"It's all right, beautiful. Take your time," he said gently.

"We went to the river," she continued. "It was a nice ride, with Nathaniel chattering in my ear the whole way. It was sweet. When we got there, I could barely get his clothes off before he jumped into the water! He splashed around like crazy, squealing like a pig. He was so dear."

Rebekah's expression softened at the memory. He could practically feel the love she had for her baby brother. It was like the emotion emanated from her spiritual being. Sweet, pure love for this precious little boy.

"Nathaniel was in the water for quite some time before I dragged him out for a lunch break. We sat together and ate the food we had brought with us for lunch. Cheese and bread were his favorite, so that's what I had packed for him. Also gingerbread. He loved that as much as I did! He devoured his lunch, and then begged to go back into the water. I made him wait a while first. I didn't want him to get sick. I tried to distract him as much as I could, getting him to take a short walk around, getting him to talk about other things, but he kept pleading to go back into the water. So finally, I let him go back into the river."

Rebekah's expression hardened, and a cold chill went through Gregory. Suddenly, he no longer wanted to hear what she was going to say. If she stopped speaking now, Nathaniel would remain a happy, bubbly three-year-old child.

Oh, please don't tell me something happened to your precious baby brother.

"I watched him splash around in the water for a bit, and then I turned around to pack up our lunch things."

Rebekah paused for what felt like an eternity. Gregory felt sick to his stomach, his entire body tense and knotted up with fear. He both wanted and dreaded to know what happened.

"I—I lost ... l—l—lost track of time," she said. Each word now was a tremendous effort. It sounded as if she couldn't catch her breath, but of course she had no breath. Her pure emotional trauma made it difficult to speak.

"I—I wasn't looking at him. I was packing up our things and wasn't paying attention. I got distracted. I was ... s—s—sin ... s—s—sin—"

He leaned forward, trying hard to understand what she was trying to tell him. Suddenly, the answer came to him.

"Singing," he finished gently for her.

"Y—yes. I was *singing*," Rebekah said angrily. "Singing. So obsessed with my own goddamned singing voice that I wasn't looking after Nathaniel. When I finally turned around after God knows how long, I couldn't see him."

Gregory's blood ran colder as he listened.

"All I could see was the ripples of the river. There was no sign of Nathaniel. No splashing, no giggling, no shouting. Nothing. Oh God, those few minutes I spent searching for him felt like hours. I'd never been so terrified in my life."

Gregory held his breath, his entire body tense. It almost felt like he was there in that moment with her. How terrifying those awful moments must have been.

"And then I saw him ... floating face down in the water."

Rebekah let out a primal shriek of grief. Her ghostly body convulsed with tearless sobs. The tragedy might have happened yesterday, so raw was her pain.

Sudden fury rose up in him, so strong and powerful that his own body shook. He wanted to scream and curse at the God who had not only allowed this horrible tragedy to occur, but who also made it physically impossible to grab Rebekah and hold her tight during a time like this.

You can hear her weeping as she walks.

"Rebekah, Rebekah," he said, trying to be heard over the sound of her sobs. When she quieted slightly, he said, "Rebekah, I'm so sorry that happened to you."

"It didn't happen to me. I made it happen. I killed him!"

"Sweetheart, it was an accident. Of course you didn't kill him. You *loved* him. You would never do anything in the world to hurt him, or anyone else."

"I did love him, but that doesn't matter. I killed him, I killed him, I killed him!" Her sobs became more distressed and wracked with grief.

As Rebekah became more hysterical, Gregory only became calmer. He was determined to do anything he could to comfort her.

"You didn't kill him. It was an accident. A terrible, tragic accident," he told her repeatedly.

"Th—then ... then I had to travel all that way back home ... I had to tell my moth ... moth—" Rebekah was so traumatized she could barely speak.

"Shhh, it's all right. You don't have to relive it."

"I relive it every day," she said, her eyes wild with grief.

The true magnitude of what she was saying crashed into him with tidal-wave force. She had been wandering, suffering, and grieving for more than two and a half centuries. The thought of it was unbearable. Unimaginable.

"I felt like I was dead after that happened," she said. "I couldn't look at anyone. I barely spoke. We had a church service for Nathaniel. We buried him. The pain was ..." Rebekah trailed off, staring into the distance. "There aren't words."

A searing agony tore through his own heart. More than anything, he wanted to reach into her soul, pull out the darkness of her grief, and bear it for her. But he couldn't. All he could do was bear witness to her torture.

"I held on for a few weeks, but I reached a point where I simply couldn't take it anymore. The grief. The guilt. The shame."

Rebekah's eyes glazed over and, for the first time since Gregory had known her, she actually looked *dead*.

Speaking in a dull, monotone voice, she said, "So I walked back to the James River and drowned myself."

Gregory's eyes welled up with tears. He couldn't remember the last time he had cried. Rebekah's tale was the saddest thing he had ever heard. He would have felt that way even if he didn't love her. Even if this horrific tragedy had happened to a stranger, his heart would have ached. But it wasn't a stranger. It was the woman he loved.

"Oh, Gregory," she lamented as she watched him wipe his tears.

"Rebekah, I'm so sorry for everything you've been through," he said, gazing into her soft gray eyes. She no longer looked dead, but her face was still full of anguish. "My God, how could you ever think I would stop loving you for a thing like this?"

She let out a choked sob, and he could see the relief in her eyes.

"But I know you stopped loving yourself on that terrible day. It was an *accident*, Rebekah." He vowed to never stop saying the words "it was an accident" to her. He would say it a million times if that's what it took to make her believe it, because it was the truth.

When she had first begun telling her terrible story, he had wondered if perhaps she had drowned trying to save her little brother. The truth was so much sadder.

"Are you sorry you did it?" Gregory asked.

"What? Killed my brother?" Rebekah asked, a bitter edge to her voice.

Calmly, he said, "You didn't kill your brother. It was an accident. I meant, are you sorry you … ended your life?"

Rebekah stared off into the distance again as she pondered the question.

"They don't say 'commit suicide' anymore," she said. "They say a person 'died by suicide.' I like that better. Committing sounds like you've committed a crime."

She fell silent for a few moments before speaking again.

"People say killing yourself is selfish. I hate that. They say you don't care about the people you leave behind, but that's not how it works. You do it, you die by suicide, because the pain you're in is so terrible you just want it to stop."

"That makes sense," Gregory said.

Rebekah turned to face him, looking surprised. He knew she feared he would judge her for what she had done, though he would never do that. He hadn't been there. He hadn't endured what she had endured. He knew he had no business saying whether it was right or wrong.

"I am sorry for my family's pain," she said. "To lose two children ... It's unimaginable. Nowadays, people talk about how common it was to lose children back in colonial times. Medicine back then wasn't what it is today, people didn't live as long, and all that. That's true, but the pain is the same. It was no easier back then to lose a child than it is now. I can't say that I'm sorry I took my own life, because I didn't deserve to live after what I'd done. My baby brother was dead, so I deserved to be dead, too."

Gregory fought the urge to contradict her, to tell her how wrong that was, but he held his tongue. He wanted to give her space to say everything she needed to say.

"I was there for my own memorial service. My God," she whispered. Gregory watched her face as she mentally relived what it was like to see her parents, her sister, and the rest of her loved ones say their final goodbyes to her. He shuddered when he remembered how close his own family had come to enduring that nightmare. If not for Rebekah, his parents might have had to bury him after he had died from diabetes complications.

"After that, once I figured out how to vanish, I did. For a long time. I didn't come back to consciousness until everyone I had known and loved was dead. I just couldn't watch them from afar. I couldn't bear to see their suffering."

"I understand," Gregory said.

"What are you thinking right now?" she asked, her eyes full of worry.

"I'm thinking I've never wanted to hold anyone as bad as I want to hold you right now," he responded without hesitation. "I'm thinking that I love you more than I thought it was possible to love anyone. And I'm thinking that I wish to God in Heaven that there was something, *anything*, I could do to take your pain away."

Rebekah smiled, and an intense relief swept through him. He'd never been more grateful to see someone smile.

"It was an accident," he said.

"Why do you keep saying that?" she asked, shaking her head.

"Because it was. And I'm gonna keep saying it until you finally come to realize that it's the truth. You can't define your whole life by your worst moment. Rebekah, I could tell how much you loved Nathaniel the first time you told me about him. Nathaniel *knows* you love him. Do you think this is what he would want for you? Eternal suffering over his death?"

"No. He wouldn't want that for me. Because he is dear and good and wonderful."

"Just like his big sister."

Rebekah scoffed at that. Gregory thought about Nathaniel as she had described him earlier. A bright, happy child who adored his big sister. And she had doted on him completely. She was also dear and good and wonderful. He had no doubts about that, but he had no idea how to convince her of it.

"I'm so glad you told me all of this, Rebekah. I can't imagine what it's been like carrying this burden all alone. Do you feel better that you told me?"

She shrugged at first, but then she nodded. "Yes. Yes, I think I do. I'm just glad you don't ..."

"I told you I could never hate you. I love you more than ever."

She appeared doubtful, but she smiled again.

"My sister had a baby," Gregory said. "A little girl. You know how it is with an infant, how exhausted and overwhelmed new moms can feel."

She nodded, no doubt remembering her little brother as an infant.

"One day Lissy, that's my sister, was gonna take the baby out for a walk in the stroller. She was tired and in a bad mood. Lack of sleep, no doubt. Anyway, she was in a hurry and she shoved the stroller too hard against the bottom door frame. The baby carrier must not have been locked into place, because it came loose. The baby carrier slammed, facedown, hard onto the pavement."

Rebekah's mouth opened wide in a soundless gasp. She looked horrified.

"It's okay," he said gently. "My niece is twelve years old now, and she's fine."

Rebekah placed her hand over her heart, looking relieved.

"My sister freaked out of course. She screamed and flipped the baby carrier over, terrified at what she would find. Lissy was so panicked that to this day, she can't remember unbuckling the baby from the carrier to pick her up, but it must have been buckled because little Katie was fine."

"Thank God for that."

"Lissy said that was the scariest moment of her life. The baby was okay, but Lissy still talks about that day. What could have happened. She's quite aware she could easily have been one of those mothers who say things like, 'My daughter would have been twelve years old today, if ...'"

Rebekah nodded, eyes filled with sadness.

"You know what the difference is between you and my sister?"

She shook her head.

"Me neither. Lissy made an innocent mistake, just like you did. She loves her daughter just like you love your brother. She would never do anything intentionally to hurt anyone, let alone a precious child. You both had accidents, and her baby lived, and your brother died. I don't know why that happened. I wish I had the answers. The only thing I know is that my sister is a good person, worthy of love, who made a mistake. Just like you."

He watched as Rebekah took in his words. He hoped he was getting through.

"Do you think Lissy is a terrible person?" he asked.

"Gregory! Of course not."

He shot her a look as if to say, "Do you see my point?"

She shrugged wearily and nodded. It was a start.

"I love that you're so calm," she said. "I know you said it used to annoy your ex-wife, but I love it. I'm such a mess inside, but having you beside me does help. Even when I'm a crying, sobbing mess, you're calm and gentle. It helps."

"I'm glad," he said. It felt good to know she loved him just the way he was.

"It's getting late," she said. "You need to go home and get some rest."

"I don't want to leave. I can stay with you tonight."

"No. I won't have it. You spend enough time here. It's getting dark, and this is no place for you to be tonight. I want you to go home."

"Yes, dear."

That got a big, unexpected laugh from Rebekah. It was a beautiful, welcome sound.

"You sound like a husband."

"*Your* husband."

"If only," she said softly. She stood up, and Gregory knew it was time for him to go. He knew from past experiences with her that if he resisted, she would simply disappear into thin air, leaving him no reason to stay.

"I'll go home, only because you're forcing me to."

Gregory stood up and gazed down at her fondly.

"Thank you for telling me all of this. I know it wasn't easy. Sweetheart, what happened to your brother was an accident. It was a terrible tragedy, but it was an accident. I love you. I will always love you, no matter what happens. You're not alone in this. Not anymore. Not ever again."

"I'm tired of being like this. I'm so, so tired," she admitted wearily.

"I know. That's why it's time to put an end to it. We're gonna figure this out. Together."

He pressed his fingers to her lips. She smiled, and then she disappeared.

18

Rebekah normally vanished for the night, but tonight she didn't. There was so much to think about that, for once, she was grateful for the time alone.

She wandered the dark streets of Williamsburg, lost in her thoughts. She could hardly believe she had told Gregory everything that had happened. Until tonight, she had never spoken to anyone, living or dead, about what she had done to Nathaniel. After she'd had to tell her family what had become of her precious little brother, she never spoke about the tragedy again. Her family had been, understandably, too grief-stricken to deal with her. After his death, she hadn't stayed around long enough to know if her family, friends, and neighbors hated her for what she had done.

Even during the years and years of wandering the Earth as a spirit, Rebekah never told anyone what had happened. She'd had some friends during that time. During both the Revolutionary War and even the Civil War, there had been no shortage of dead soldiers to befriend after the terrible battles that had occurred here. Though most of the fallen went to their reward immediately after being killed in battle, there were still many left behind. Over the years, they had somehow come to terms with whatever trauma or heartache had kept them here. Eventually, all her friends went away. Existence as a ghost was lonely enough, and she'd always felt she couldn't take the risk of confessing she had murdered a child to anyone, lest she lose the few friends she had.

It was an accident.

Gregory's words echoed in her ears. She didn't believe those words. It was her own selfishness and carelessness that had cost Nathaniel his life. Even so, Rebekah couldn't forget the gentle concern on Gregory's face when he spoke. He had asked if she felt better after confessing to him. At the time, she wasn't sure. Her emotions were too raw. Now, though, she was sure.

Yes. She did feel better. Much better.

It was harder to hate herself when he looked at her the way he did. With pure love, compassion, and understanding.

Usually when she walked through the streets alone at night, she obsessed over all the terrible memories of the past. Tonight, she allowed herself to think of happy memories. Like the day Nathaniel was born. How she and Martha had fallen in love with him at first sight. As an infant, he didn't cry that much. Rebekah's mother had said both she and Martha had been terrible babies. They never slept well and were often irritable and fussy. Nathaniel was naturally calm. Well, he was calm in the sense that he was rarely unhappy and didn't throw tantrums. He was excitable, though, in a good way. Rebekah chuckled to herself, remembering how difficult it had been to keep that little boy quiet at church.

She found herself smiling as she remembered his happy little laugh, and the way he squealed when he was excited. She even relished the memory of the sight and sound of Nathaniel splashing happily in the James River. For just a moment, Rebekah allowed herself to believe she had meant well. All she had wanted was to give him a happy day because she loved him. In the days leading up to the trip, he'd been so excited, he could barely sleep.

"I only wanted to bring you joy," she said in a soft voice. "I'm so sorry."

Rebekah tried to focus on the happy memories of her family, but the horrific details of that awful day always came crashing back. Those horrible, panic-stricken moments when she desperately searched for her brother in the water. The terror that had clutched her heart when she saw him floating in the river. The otherworldly sound of her own scream when she'd realized what she had done. The way his tiny, limp body felt in her arms. His heart and his breath had stopped, but he had still been warm. In a fit of panic and grief, she had fainted. When she'd awoken to face her living nightmare, she had wrapped his tiny body in the picnic blanket. Then she'd faced the agonizing horseback ride back home, knowing she would have to tell her family the unthinkable.

She began to sob openly at the memories. She quickly turned invisible, lest she add more credence to the lore of the Weeping Woman.

Rebekah calmed herself by picturing Gregory's face. Things were different now. She wasn't alone anymore. She had Gregory now, and he still loved her.

She headed back toward Hay's Cabinetmaker's Shop without consciously realizing where she was going. She sat down in the grass near the bridge where she and Gregory had sat together earlier in the evening. An unfamiliar sense of peace settled over her. Rehashing the trauma of that day had been terrible, but she was truly grateful that he had forced her to do it. He had been horrified all right, because he was a good, caring person. It was terrible to hear about the tragic death of an innocent child.

The strange thing was the way he'd looked horrified that she was blaming herself for what had happened. Rebekah clearly recalled his initial reaction to her story. Dark eyes wide, he'd exclaimed, "Sweetheart, it was an accident!"

She appreciated his compassionate response, but she wasn't sure she deserved it. She recalled Gregory's story about his sister. It was so easy to imagine how it had happened.

Rebekah's heart caught in her throat as she imagined what those few seconds must have felt like. The mother watching in horror as the baby carrier popped out of the stroller and flipped, landing on the ground face down. Her hand flew to her mouth even now just recalling the story Gregory had relayed. Rebekah knew exactly how his sister must have felt as she, hands probably shaking, had picked up the baby carrier, not knowing what she would find. The child could have been bloodied, tiny skull crushed.

The baby could have been dead.

Rebekah tried to steady her emotions, reminding herself the baby was fine.

Not a baby anymore, she thought. Now she was a perfectly healthy preteen girl, thank the sweet Lord.

She was nowhere near ready to forgive herself for

Nathaniel's death. She likely never would be. But she could see Gregory's point. Lissy wasn't evil. She was a loving, exhausted, *human* mother, capable of both extreme love and awful mistakes. Rebekah could never have blamed Lissy if harm had come to the child.

Gregory had given her a lot to think about.

19

Rebekah caught sight of Orlando the next morning as she walked toward Hay's to see Gregory. She was still invisible.

Might as well get this over with.

She figured he must have a lot of questions about her being dead. After discreetly ducking behind the Apothecary building to turn visible, she headed toward him. His dark brown eyes opened wide at the sight of her. He was dressed in his usual Williamsburg getup; tricorn hat and woolen coat. He was handsome as always, but for once, Rebekah wasn't looking forward to talking to him. She wasn't angry with Gregory anymore about telling Orlando the truth about her. After all, she had been the one to insist he spend time with man. Still, she really hated having people know she was dead.

"Hello, Orlando," Rebekah said with a smile.

"Hello," he responded a bit uncertainly. At least he wasn't shrinking back in horror.

He stared at her, and she patiently waited for him to make the first move.

"Is it true? What Gregory said about you?" he asked, his eyes still wide.

"Yes."

Orlando still stared at her. Rebekah was dimly aware of tourists beginning to fill the streets as the historical buildings were about to open. Duke of Gloucester Street was no place to have this particular discussion.

"Come with me," she said, heading back to the area behind the Apothecary building located on a small side street off the Palace Green. Orlando dutifully followed behind.

Once they were safely hidden, Rebekah turned to face him.

"Yes. What Gregory told you about me is true. I'm dead. Have been for a long time."

Saying the words out loud made her feel better, which took her by surprise. Perhaps it was because Orlando already knew about her, and she was simply confirming it. Yet, there was more to it than that. She realized how tired she was of keeping secrets. Being dead and being haunted by tragic memories was exhausting and lonely. It helped to have Gregory, and now Orlando, to share her troubles with.

"Wow," he said, looking her up and down. Then he looked into her eyes. "Can I, you know, touch you?"

"Yes. You can reach out and try to touch me. As long as you promise not to scream or faint or throw up."

"What kind of wuss do you think I am?"

"That's what I'm trying to figure out," she teased.

Orlando laughed, and she felt good all over. Joking with him was fun, and it made her feel normal.

"Orlando," she said, gently but firmly. "You really won't be able to touch me. Your hand will go right through my body. Do you understand that?"

"I think so," he said. Rebekah appreciated his honesty. It was hard to wrap one's mind around such things.

"Okay."

Rebekah slowly extended her arm with her palm up toward him. She didn't touch him, though. She thought it best for him to reach out for her when he was ready. Orlando stretched out his hand and placed it on top of hers as if he was placing something in her palm. As she'd warned, his hand went straight through hers.

He gasped and took a step back.

She understood, of course, but it still hurt to see Orlando's handsome face recoil. She gave him a moment to recover before speaking.

"Please don't be scared of me," she said wearily.

His expression softened. He could probably tell she was upset.

"I—I'm not. I'm just, you know, kind of getting used to the idea, that's all." He looked at her curiously but didn't seem afraid. "So, you died in 1760-something?"

"1762."

"How did you die?"

Her face fell.

"Oh, I'm sorry. I shouldn't ask personal questions like that."

"It's all right," she reassured him. "There's hardly an etiquette book to follow for a thing like this. I drowned."

"Oh, right. You're the Weeping—"

Orlando stopped short, looking embarrassed. Rebekah laughed. She couldn't help it.

"Yes. I am the Weeping Woman." She smiled warmly at him.

He smiled gratefully back at her. More than anything,

she wanted to put him at ease. He was a good friend to Gregory, and she liked to think of him as her friend, too.

"You were really young," he said sadly. "I'm sorry that happened to you."

"Thank you," she said, hoping he wouldn't ask any more questions about her death.

"Wow. You're really dead. That sucks."

She laughed. "Yes, it rather does."

"Well, at least you died wearing a pretty dress. You look beautiful. I never would have known, you know, if Gregory hadn't told me."

Rebekah lowered her head shyly. "Thank you for saying that. It means a lot."

"You and Gregory seem so perfect for each other. All this time, he kept saying you were 'unavailable,' and that it couldn't ever work between you two. I couldn't figure out what could possibly be keeping you apart. I thought you might be married or something."

"Oh, no. The only person I've ever wanted to marry is Gregory."

Orlando sighed heavily. "He's such a good guy. He deserves to be happy. And so do you."

She shrugged, not really believing that last part. "Gregory certainly does deserve to be happy. He's trying so hard to help me cross over, but I don't want to leave him."

Rebekah had been wandering the Earth as a spirit for so long, it had always seemed impossible she would ever make it to Heaven. She recalled the odd sense of peace that had settled over her yesterday when thinking about her brother and everything that had happened. After experiencing that strange sense of calm, for once it seemed possible that she might make it to the other side.

And the thought terrified her.

"I don't want him to be alone," Rebekah said with a quiver in her voice. "I love him so much."

"I know," Orlando said. "I can tell."

"It wouldn't seem fair to leave him."

"Yeah. I get that. But Gregory loves you, and I know he just wants you to find peace. That's the most important thing to him."

Rebekah nodded. "Yes. He's like that. So completely unselfish. But the idea of leaving him behind is unbearable."

She stopped speaking, knowing that if she went on, she would start to cry.

"The last thing Gregory would want is for you to stay behind just for him."

"True," she said, somehow managing to collect herself. "I'm so sorry, Orlando. I didn't mean to burden you like this."

"It's okay. Gregory needed to talk about it with somebody, and I guess you do, too."

"I must say, you're handling this whole me-being-dead-thing pretty well."

"I am a man of faith," he said with pride and conviction. "I guess it's not all that surprising to me that there's life after death." Orlando thought for a moment. "You know, if you make it ... I mean, *when* you make it to Heaven, I bet you'll be able to watch over Gregory."

Rebekah said softly, "I hope so."

"People say you can get messages from people in Heaven. Like they send you coins and butterflies and stuff like that to show they are okay and that they're watching over you. I really like to believe that's true."

"You lost someone close to you, didn't you?" Rebekah asked, although she already knew the answer.

"My mother. I was only seven years old."

"My heart breaks for you," Rebekah said. It felt good to finally have the chance to tell him how sorry she was for his grief.

"Thanks. Maybe you'll see her. When the time comes."

"Maybe. I hope so."

"This is gonna sound really dumb," he said with an uncomfortable laugh. "But if you do see her, tell her, you know ... tell her ..."

"You want me to tell her that you love her," Rebekah said gently, making sure to meet his gaze.

"Yeah. Tell her I love her, and I miss her every single day."

"If I'm lucky enough to get the chance to meet your mother, I will absolutely tell her that, Orlando."

"Thank you."

"She must be so proud of you."

"I can only hope. Well, I guess I better get on to work."

"Okay. If you haven't already, would you mind not telling anyone else about me?"

"Oh yeah, no problem. No, I haven't said a word to anybody, and I promise I won't."

"I appreciate that," she said with relief. Not only did she hate the idea of people knowing she was dead, but having people know she was the Weeping Woman would make it a lot harder for her to be with Gregory out in public.

"I just wish there was something I could do for you and Gregory."

"Maybe there is."

"Name it," he said firmly, looking her in the eye.

"Be there for him," she said, her voice breaking already. "In case I do go away. Please. Promise me you'll be there for him. Take care of him for me."

"I will, Rebekah. I swear to you."

She felt better that Gregory wouldn't be totally alone if she made it to the other side.

"It was really nice talking to you, Orlando."

"You too," he said.

She turned and hurried to see Gregory, hoping that Ben wasn't working today so she could stay at the shop. As she got closer, she began to get nervous. Last night, he had been warm and kind after hearing the sordid details of her life. What if he'd changed his mind after he'd had some time to think about what she had done?

She went invisible and slipped inside the shop to see if Gregory was alone. He was. She watched him gathering some carpentry tools to work on his current project, a lovely chair. Not wanting to invade his privacy, she turned visible. He didn't even flinch.

"Good morning, darling," he said, looking up and flashing her a sexy grin.

"Good morning. No Ben today?"

"Nope."

"Good."

Gregory nodded. "How are you feeling? I've been so worried about you. I hate seeing you upset."

"I'm all right. I think it did help to talk about it. I didn't think that it would, but it did. I'm glad you made me tell you."

"Glad to hear it," he said, looking relieved.

"I spoke to Orlando this morning."

Gregory wrinkled his nose, wincing. "Oh. How did that go?"

Rebekah playfully tapped him on the nose. If the cold bothered him, he didn't show it.

"I proved to him you were telling the truth about me,"

she said as she dragged her hand through Gregory's body. This time, he did shiver a little.

"Sorry. It went fine with Orlando."

"He wasn't afraid?"

"No, not really. Took a little bit to adjust, I suppose, but by the end of our talk, it felt like I was speaking with an old friend. It was nice."

"That's good," he said. Rebekah stifled a laugh when she heard the irritation in his voice. It was silly of Gregory to be jealous of Orlando, but she couldn't help being flattered.

"Will you play the harpsichord for me?" she asked, knowing that was the best way to boost Gregory's confidence. That, and she genuinely did want to hear him play.

"Sure," he said with a sexy smile.

He sat down at the harpsichord and launched into "Two Quick Steps and a Dance Medley," which he knew was one of her favorites. It was an upbeat, cheery tune, and it lifted her spirits greatly. It also pleased her to watch Gregory's face as he played.

Oh, he's so handsome.

How could he for a moment ever think she could prefer Orlando to him?

"That was lovely," she said when Gregory finished the song. "Thank you, darling."

"My pleasure," he said. He frowned for a moment, looking as if he was concentrating on something.

"What's the matter?" she asked.

He turned to look at her. "I have an idea."

"Okay ..." she said, waiting for him to continue.

"You might get mad at me."

"It's certainly possible," she teased.

"I think it might help you in your path to crossing over ... I think it would be good if you started singing again."

Pain stabbed at her heart as she was, once again, thrust back into the awful day of Nathaniel's death. Shame overwhelmed her, knowing that Gregory was aware that her selfish singing had been the reason her brother had drowned.

"I know it's hard," he said gently. He gazed at her with concern at seeing how difficult this was for her. "But I really believe this can help you."

Sudden fear at the notion of leaving him forever gripped her. She felt like screaming *I don't want to go.*

"Well, maybe I don't want to be helped!" Rebekah snapped back. "Why can't you just let this go?"

She was suddenly furious at the whole notion of Gregory forcing her to try to cross over. She had been just fine before he had showed up. Why couldn't he leave her alone?

Fresh pain seared her heart. She knew she wasn't really angry with Gregory, and that the last thing she wanted was to be mean to him. In truth, she was agonizing over the thought of having to leave him behind. And, when it came down to it, she knew she still didn't deserve to go to Heaven.

Gregory remained calm and soothing as always.

"I know this must be hard, Rebekah. But it's gonna be okay. Everything's gonna be okay."

She gazed into his sweet brown eyes. He understood she was lashing out because she was afraid. Every time she got overly emotional, he responded with thoughtful, quiet wisdom.

"Why are you so kind to me?"

"Because I love you. I know you don't think you're worthy of crossing over, but I'm not going to stop until you change your mind. Someday you're going to understand, *really understand*, that what happened was an accident.

You'll come to understand that in life, and in death, you've been an incredible, loving woman. A sister, a daughter, a friend. And a lover, as much as that's possible for you right now. I love you. And someday, you'll learn to love yourself. And when that happens, you'll finally make it to the other side."

Rebekah heard the catch in Gregory's voice as he spoke.

"I don't want to leave you."

"I know. But that's the way it has to be. We both know that." Gregory glanced at the harpsichord, and then back at her. "You said you used to sing for your family, right?"

"Yes."

"I bet they loved hearing you sing," he said.

"They did," Rebekah admitted. "I remember ..."

She stopped, struggling to get her emotions under control.

"Take your time," he encouraged.

"At my funeral service, my father said, 'Oh, how we'll miss her song.'"

"After what happened to me that day you saved my life, I kept thinking what my parents would have done if I had died. My God, your parents must have been heartbroken when they lost you," he said, shaking his head.

"They were." It was true. She had seen it herself. The agony in the eyes of her mother, father, and sister at her memorial service. It had been unbearable.

"I know you won't sing for yourself. Do it for them. Rebekah, I know they can see and hear you from where they are. I really believe that. If you sing for them, they'll know. Your mother. Your father. Your sister. Your *brother*. Sing for them, sweetheart."

Overcome with emotion and unable to speak just yet, she considered his words. She had never thought about singing as a tribute to her loved ones. For an eternity she had regretted her actions. Agonized over everything she had put her family through when she had taken her own life. Perhaps singing for them now was a small way to express her love for them.

"Yes," she whispered. "I'll do it. I'll do it for them."

"Tell me what to play for you."

"How about a song of praise? I used to sing hymns a lot for my family. I think that would be a fitting way to start."

"That sounds perfect."

Rebekah thought for a moment. "Do you know 'All Creatures of Our God and King?'"

"Not offhand, but lemme check to see if I can find the music. I know I have a bunch of hymnals here."

Gregory rifled around through a wooden box filled with sheet music that sat beside the harpsichord. Rebekah felt apprehensive about singing, the traumatic memories of the last time she sang still fresh in her mind. She reminded herself why she was doing this. She would sing in honor of her family and in praise of the God who had given her many blessings in life and even in death.

"If I can't find it, I can always look it up on the Inter— Ah ha! Got it!"

Rebekah giggled at his enthusiasm, and her nerves calmed. Gregory, her departed loved ones, and God Almighty were as supportive an audience as one could get. They wouldn't mind if she got some notes wrong. They knew what was in her heart.

"Ready?"

"I think so," she said with a quiver in her voice.

"Don't overthink it, love. Just go for it."

With that, he started playing the hymn before she had a chance to change her mind. Out of habit, she tried to draw in a deep breath, but of course none came. She didn't need to breathe to sing or to speak as a ghost.

Closing her eyes, she began to sing as loud and strong as she could. She was a tad rusty at first, but soon she found herself reaching the familiar notes with ease.

"All creatures of our God and King, lift up your voice and with us sing Alleluia! Alleluia! Thou burning sun with golden beam.Thou silver moon with softer gleam. Oh, praise Him, Oh, praise Him, Alleluia! Alleluia! Alleluia!"

A strange combination of calm and elation coursed through her spirit form. She had thoroughly expected to feel terrible as she sang. She had prepared herself for feelings of worthlessness and shame to crash over her. A tiny part of her feared she would even be committing a sin if she dared sing again. The sin of pride, wanting Gregory to admire her voice. The sin of selfishly taking part in a pleasurable activity that had once cost her brother his life.

Rebekah launched into the next verses of the song, and her feeling of joy remained. Intensified, even. No, this didn't feel like sin. It was the opposite. Her song was a prayer of gratitude and of love and joy. She hoped with all her heart that her family could hear her.

This is for you, Mama and Papa. And for you, Martha and dear, sweet Nathaniel.

By the time she had finished singing, she had forgotten Gregory was even in the room, even though he supplied the accompaniment for her song.

She opened her eyes and gazed down at Gregory where he sat on the wooden bench. His eyes were shining with happiness, which only reinforced her notion that she had done the right thing by singing after all these years.

"Rebekah, that was beautiful. Just *beautiful*. Everything I expected and even more. But more importantly, how do you feel?"

"Better. Singing for my family makes me feel like they're here with me again. I had forgotten how much I loved to sing. How calming and healing it is."

"Music is like that," Gregory said softly.

Rebekah let out a breathless sigh, reveling in the deep connection their souls shared.

"Yes, it certainly is. There's a song. A special song I made up just for my brother, but I don't think I'm ready to do that one yet."

"I understand. You're doing great, Rebekah. Do you want to try another one?"

"Yes, I would! Something happy and upbeat. How about something from *The Beggar's Opera*?"

"Coming right up," he said, shuffling his music.

The Beggar's Opera was a popular show that had frequently been performed in her day. It was a satire of opera, and it had a lot of catchy tunes. Gregory knew a lot of songs from that show.

"How about this one?" he asked, holding up the page of music for the song "Youth's the Season Made for Joy."

"Perfect."

A ripple of excitement went through Rebekah as she prepared to sing again. It was a delightful sensory reminder of the way she had felt in life. Singing had always been such an emotional release that made her feel good all over. And dear God, it had been a long time since she had sung anything. Two and a half centuries.

She had a high, light voice, and this song showed off her range nicely. This time, she was able to enjoy Gregory's reaction to hearing her sing. Rebekah watched him grin as he played the harpsichord. Oh, what a joy it was to share in his music. Yet another way to feel connected to him.

She made sure to sing her very best, watching him the whole time. When she finished, she received a round of applause, and it wasn't from him. She had been so preoccupied by singing for Gregory, she hadn't even noticed the group of tourists that had wandered in. Pride swelled in Rebekah at first, but she felt the familiar surge of guilt return.

She lowered her head, a gesture that might have been mistaken for shyness by the listeners. Terrible images of Nathaniel's little body returned to her mind, and Rebekah knew there was no getting rid of them. Ever.

"Don't stop on our account," a young woman said. "We'd love to hear another one."

"Come on, Rebekah," Gregory said, looking up at her until she was forced to meet his gaze. "Let's do another one."

His tone was gentle, and his eyes were full of love and encouragement. He could tell her faith in herself was faltering, and, as always, he was right by her side to lift her up. Had they been alone, Rebekah probably would have refused to sing again. But they weren't alone. There were tourists here now, and it was Gregory's job to entertain them. She couldn't let him down.

"How about the Shakespearean songbook?" Rebekah suggested, forcing herself to sound cheerful. She wondered if she would be able to recapture the joy she had felt just a few moments ago. She also wondered if she deserved to.

"Good idea," Gregory said, grabbing the sheet music she'd suggested. There were a number of Shakespearean passages that had been set to music, and she was familiar with many of them, as she had heard him play the music for tourists many times over the last few months. Until now, there had been no one around to sing the lyrics. "This is a nice one."

"Yes, it is."

Gregory had chosen "Under the Greenwood Tree" from *As You Like It*. It was a good song that would show off her soprano voice. Rebekah sang along with Gregory's expert harpsichord playing. It took a few verses, but the healing magic of the music began to calm her again. Her mother had once referred to her voice as a gift from God, and that was how Rebekah tried to think of singing now. Sharing her gift as God had intended.

At the conclusion of the song, the tourists applauded again and thanked them. Rebekah did enjoy the warm smiles on their faces. It reminded her of how she had felt when she allowed Harry to catch a glimpse of her spirit form. Making people happy felt good. So much of being a ghost involved feeling utterly useless. Her singing had made people smile today, if only for a moment. Yes. That was truly a special gift.

Two older couples entered the building just after the younger tourists left. Gregory pointed to "Ariel's Song" from *The Tempest*, and Rebekah nodded. He began to play, and she started to sing. The four older tourists lingered to hear the music. Rebekah caught the eye of one of the women, who smiled warmly at her. The kind look on the lady's face reminded Rebekah of her grandmother, filling her with more warm memories of her family.

Throughout the morning, a steady stream of tourists came through the shop, and Gregory and Rebekah entertained them with their songs. When a group of teenagers came in, Gregory began to play a Taylor Swift song on the harpsichord. Rebekah giggled, and so did the teens. Modern music sounded funny on the harpsichord. Rebekah knew the words to the song because she'd heard it played often in the College of William and Mary dorms. She sang the lyrics in an over-the-top soprano voice, and delighted, Gregory threw back his head and laughed, nearly missing a few notes on the harpsichord.

The teenagers applauded when they finished the song. More warmth and joy spread through Rebekah as she surveyed their smiling faces. When the youngsters left, there was finally a lull in the foot traffic.

Gregory turned to her. "See? That's another reason why it's good to sing again. It makes people happy. It's something really amazing you can still do, even being the way you are."

"I'm glad of that," she said.

"You're such a good woman, Rebekah. You really are."

Reveling in the warmth of the human contact she'd been blessed with today, Rebekah smiled. It made her feel perhaps she wasn't utterly horrible after all.

20

Gregory noticed a change in Rebekah right after she confided in him about her tragic life. The change hadn't happened overnight, but it was noticeable. Over the last several weeks, her demeanor had calmed and her emotions had become more stable. She had been able to talk about her brother's tragic drowning without crying, and her self-hatred had seemed to lessen. Gregory's assurance of his love seemed to help. He still couldn't believe she thought he would hate her for what had happened.

That showed how hard she was on herself. Upon hearing of the tragedy, any rational person would have had nothing but compassion for Rebekah after having been through something like that. Anyone could see that Nathaniel's death was a horrific accident. Nobody except Rebekah herself would think she was a monster.

"You seem to be doing a lot better," he commented as they stood inside the shop one afternoon.

There was still sorrow in her eyes, but that awful,

distressed look on her face appeared less and less these days.

Rebekah nodded sadly.

"It's a good thing, sweetie."

"I know."

"I've been trying to think of things that might help you even more," Gregory said. "Do you ever go back to the river?"

"Yes. I've gone back a few times over the years. Going back there ... is very difficult for me. People nowadays call it a trigger. It triggers me to go there. Makes me spiral down into a horrible depression that can last for weeks. When I visit the river, sometimes it feels like it's happening all over again. It feels so real. Like it was yesterday and not years and years ago."

Gregory hated to force her to confront such painful memories, but he was pretty sure it was the only way she would ever find peace.

"I'm not sure it would help for me to go there again."

"I think it might," he said.

Rebekah winced at the mere idea, and he knew he had to tread carefully. He wanted to help, but he didn't want to act like he knew what she was going through, because he didn't. It was one thing to offer advice, but it was quite another to be the one to actually follow it. He suppressed a sigh, wishing like hell there was some way he could endure the trauma for her. But this was something Rebekah had to face.

"I can't imagine how difficult it must be. To go back to where it happened, but I think it might be an important step. I could go with you if you think it would help."

The distressed look was back, and Gregory's heart hurt to see it.

"I'm sorry. I didn't mean to upset you."

"Do you think he's forgiven me?" she asked.

"Nathaniel?"

She nodded, her eyes full of fear.

"Yes. Of course. Where he is now," Gregory said, glancing upward for a moment, "I believe he can see into your heart. He knows you love him. He knows you'd never hurt him on purpose. And he knows how terribly sorry you are. Yes, I believe he's forgiven you. That is, if he ever even blamed you in the first place."

"What about my parents?"

"They knew how much you loved your brother, too. I can't imagine they would ever question that. In those early days after it happened, I'm sure they were too consumed with grief to talk to you. I think if you had lived longer, they would have eventually talked with you about it some, and it might have put your mind at ease."

"What about killing myself? Do you think they've forgiven me for that?"

Gregory pondered that for a moment.

"Wh—what are you thinking?"

"I was just thinking I can't imagine their pain. I was thinking how sorry I am that they had to go through this. To lose two children." Gregory gazed tenderly at her. "I'm sorry for you and your family. That you had to endure all of this. And yes, I'm sure they've forgiven you. I can't say how they felt when you died. They were probably hurt and angry. Losing you added to their pain, and I'm sure that was awful. Rebekah, I can't say what you did was right or wrong, but I'm sure your mother and father must have known you did it because losing Nathaniel in that way was too much for you to bear. They might not have agreed with your tragic decision, but I bet they at least understood it."

Rebekah looked off into the distance, pondering Gregory's words.

"There is one thing I know for sure about your family. They want you to be with them instead of being stuck here. Think about it, Rebekah. How wonderful it would be to cross over. Don't you realize you'll get to see them all again? You can tell them all yourself how sorry you are. You'll see your baby brother again. Where he is now, he's whole again. He's happy and at peace. And you'll get to see that with your own eyes. You won't have to think of him the way he was when you last saw him. You'll see him smile and laugh."

Rebekah let out a choked sob, but she nodded. Gregory knew how much she needed to see her brother again. As a person, and not as a dead body.

"Nathaniel's all right now," Gregory reassured her. "When you get to where he is, you'll see. And you won't grieve him anymore."

"Grief has been such a huge part of my existence for so long. It's hard to imagine being without it."

"But what a wonderful idea to get used to," he said.

"Oh Gregory, do you really think I'll see them again?"

"I have absolutely no doubt about it. Your loved ones are up in Heaven, and they're waiting for you to join them so the family can be complete again."

Rebekah smiled, and Gregory saw a ray of hope cut through the darkness in her eyes.

"Oh yes," he said. "You'll see them all again."

And once you're gone, I'll see you again someday, too. But I might have to wait a long, long time.

21

Rebekah had begun visiting Jennings Tavern late at night when all the tourists had gone home. It felt good to spend some quiet alone time inside the home she had shared with her family, as well as to walk the grounds outside. Of course, she had visited the tavern many times over the years, but lately it felt different when she visited. The memories were brighter, happier, more vivid. She felt more connected to her family than she had in a long time. There were moments when she could actually feel their presence.

Rebekah floated through the walls with ease, drifting into the Great Room. There were so many warm memories in this room. The drinking and laughter of the guests who stayed in the tavern, the late evening card and dice games. And, best of all, the elegant dancing parties that took place from time to time. She remembered the longing she'd felt in her heart as she watched the happy couples dance together.

Then she recalled her dance with Gregory on the day of that wedding at the Governor's Palace. She smiled at that sweet, romantic memory. A bittersweet memory, now. It had warmed her heart every time she'd thought of it, but now it was tinged with the sadness of knowing they might soon have to part.

After all, the closer she felt to her family, the farther it pushed her away from Gregory and his earthly form.

Rebekah wandered around the rest of the tavern, passing through the Bull Head Room and the public dining room. Then she headed up the stairs to the bedroom chambers. On her nightly visits to her old home, she spent the majority of her time in the sleeping quarters. That was where she had slept near Martha and Nathaniel. Being there made her recall all the bedtime stories and songs and laughter they had shared.

Over the last few visits there, she had begun speaking out loud to her brother and sister.

"I love you, Martha. I love you, Nathaniel. I miss you," she would say.

On the first night, Rebekah had felt a bit silly. That feeling had faded, and soon she felt comfortable talking to them as if they were there in the room with her. In life, when she'd had a problem, she had frequently turned to her big sister for advice. She saw no reason to stop now.

"I don't know what to do, Martha," she'd say to the empty room that didn't really feel empty. "I miss you and Nathaniel and Mama and Papa. I know I'm supposed to go home to be with you, but somehow, I feel like my home is here with Gregory. Somehow, it just feels right. Like I'm supposed to be his wife, and we're supposed to spend our lives together. But that's crazy. How can I spend my life with him when I have no life? I'm dead. Long, long dead. Why am I so confused? What am I supposed to do?"

Rebekah asked these questions nightly, until one night she got an answer.

It wasn't a response that she heard with her ears, but it was one she felt deeply in her heart. She heard the message as clear as day.

The time has come, Rebekah.

Sitting on the bed in her old bedroom, Rebekah closed her eyes. She felt a deep sense of peace and belonging on a level she had never experienced before. In that moment, she felt connected to the entire Universe.

She also felt an irresistible urge to go back to the James River.

It was time.

∽

REBEKAH WAITED for Gregory on the bridge the next morning before the shop opened. At first glance, he seemed surprised to see her. She rarely showed up before lunchtime, just in case Ben was around. On his second glance at her, she could tell that Gregory knew something was up.

"What's wrong?" he asked.

She immediately broke down into a tearless sob. After wrestling with her emotions all night, she had wanted to stay composed when she broke the news to him. She should have known it would be impossible once she saw him, knowing it would likely be the last time.

As always, Gregory stayed calm. "It's all right, beautiful. Take your time."

Gazing at him sorrowfully, she reached out to touch his face. She would have given anything to feel the touch of his skin. The warmth of his embrace. *Just once.*

"I think it's my time," she said, her voice barely a whisper.

He nodded slowly. Rebekah knew he would remain calm and steady for her sake. Oh, how cruel it was that she couldn't throw her arms around him. She couldn't kiss him goodbye.

Goodbye.

Merely thinking the word sent shockwaves of grief through her ghostly form.

"I don't want to go. I don't want to leave you," she cried.

"I know, darling," Gregory said gently. "I know. But you can't stay. You know that. This is what's supposed to happen. All your suffering. All your pain. It's almost over now."

"I'm supposed to go to the river. It's not that I want to. I just know that's what I'm supposed to do. What I *have* to do."

"Do you want me to come with you?"

She shook her head vehemently.

"It's not that I don't want you to go. I wish you could be there by my side." Rebekah gazed at him lovingly. "But I'll never be able to go where I'm supposed to go if I can still see you."

"Yeah, I think you're right," Gregory said with a weak smile. "If I were the one who had to leave, I don't think I could do it either, if you were standing right there."

Rebekah suddenly had a strong, uncontrollable urge to rush to the river.

"Oh, Gregory, I don't want to go!" Her voice was nearly a shriek.

"I know, my love, I know," he said, moving as close to her as was possible. He stared fiercely into her eyes. It hurt so badly to watch him struggle to keep from breaking down.

"I don't want you to fight it. You hear me? Rebekah, if you're given the chance, I want you to walk toward the light. You hear me? *Walk toward the light.*"

The waver in Gregory's voice nearly destroyed her.

"Promise me. Promise me!" he demanded.

"I will. I promise," she managed to say through broken sobs. "I'm so sorry I dragged you into this mess."

"Rebekah, I will never, ever regret that we met. No matter what happens, meeting you, loving you, it wasn't a mistake. I'll always be grateful for the time we spent together."

"Thank you for everything you've done for me. I never could have gotten this far without your love and support."

The pull to leave and go back to the river was nearly unbearable now. Her time was running short.

"I—I have to go," she said.

"Okay, it's okay." He still spoke calmly, but she could hear the touch of panic in his voice.

"Gregory, after I'm gone," she said, struggling mightily to get the words out, "if there's any way that I can appear to you, I will. I might be able to send messages, like showing you coins or birds or butterflies or something. So many times over the years when I've been lost in a fit of grief, I see a butterfly. I always wondered if maybe that was a message from my brother. Telling me he's okay. If I can send you a message like that from where I am, I will. I promise."

"Good. That sounds wonderful, darling," he said.

"Gregory, I—I ..." She broke down again, not even knowing what to say. There weren't words to express how much she loved him.

"It's all right, sweetheart, it's all right. Don't worry. Try not to be sad. Where you're going there will be no more pain, no more sorrow. No more grief."

"B—but you—"

"I'll be fine. Please don't worry about me."

He gently touched her lips and said, "'And whether we

shall meet again, I know not. Therefore, our everlasting farewell take. Forever and forever, farewell. If we do meet again, why, we shall smile …'"

Shakily, Rebekah managed to say the last part of the quote from Shakespeare's *Julius Caesar* with Gregory. "'If not, why then, this parting was well made.'"

"I love you, Rebekah. *Always*."

"I love you too," she said.

Then she faded from view.

22

Gregory held his expression steady after he watched Rebekah disappear. For all he knew, she was still there, watching him, invisible. He didn't want to do anything that might jeopardize her journey to the other side. If he broke down, it would be harder for her to let go of her earthly existence.

Slowly, he trudged into Hay's Cabinetmaker's Shop. Thank God Ben wasn't working today. Gregory didn't have the energy to pretend that everything was all right.

No music in the shop today. He would eventually play the harpsichord again, but he wasn't up to it yet. There were too many memories of Rebekah standing by his side as he played. Listening intently at first, then eventually singing along. Music was healing, of course. Gregory knew he would turn to music for solace at some point, but his emotions were far too raw for that right now.

He got to work on an intricate wooden chair leg, doing his best to concentrate. It wasn't easy. He had known losing Rebekah would hurt, but he wasn't prepared for it to hurt this much.

The shop seemed so quiet without her. Even on the days when she wasn't there with him, Gregory knew he could still look forward to sitting outside and having lunch with her.

There were times during this morning when he forgot, just for a few seconds, that Rebekah was gone for good. For a brief instant, he thought about what they would do that evening after work. Then he would remember she was gone. And the searing pain would grip him all over again.

It was like having his wife suddenly die. One day spending his life with his soulmate. The next day, a grief-stricken widower. Gregory's eyes filled with tears. Not only would he grieve for Rebekah for the rest of his life, but most people would never even know she had existed. He would have to bear this grief all on his own. No one would come to his house, bringing hot meals and kind words of warmth and support to help him through the early stages of grief. There would be no sympathy cards, no kind words of understanding.

Hands trembling, Gregory set down the chair back he had been working on. He was in no shape to even attempt to carve intricate woodworking designs. He was barely functioning. He felt like he wanted to die.

Now there was an idea.

It would be so easy. All he had to do was stop taking his medication. Hell, he wouldn't even have to do that. After all, he'd nearly dropped dead before by simply waiting too long to eat.

Gregory gazed around at his shop. He was all alone. Yes. It would be *so easy.*

Visions of being found dead filled his head. He winced, realizing it would likely be tourists who found him. What if they had children with them? Even if they didn't, he hated the idea of traumatizing anyone, even adults, by having them discover his dead body in the shop. Besides, if he did die, what if he wound up like Rebekah?

He chuckled bitterly at the irony. Rebekah would cross over, and he would be stuck here as a ghost. Even in death, they still wouldn't be together.

"Have I learned nothing from Shakespeare?" Gregory muttered aloud, knowing the thought would have amused Rebekah. Romeo had killed himself thinking Juliet was dead, only to have Juliet wake up and find his corpse.

Wearily, he shook his head. No. Killing himself was not the answer. His grief for Rebekah was unbearable, and the last thing he wanted was to put his parents through that.

Somehow, some way, Gregory would simply have to go on living without the love of his life.

There was nothing for him to do now but pray for Rebekah's peace.

He closed his eyes and did just that.

∽

AT LUNCHTIME, Gregory was far too depressed to even think about food, but he knew he had to force himself to eat something. He smiled weakly, knowing Rebekah would have fussed over him to make sure he had some lunch. That made the idea of eating easier. He would do it for her.

He needed some fresh air after moping around all morning, but he didn't want to go to their usual tree. Gregory stepped out of the back door of the shop, unsure of exactly where he was headed. Fresh pain squeezed his heart when he saw the bridge where he had last seen Rebekah. He realized it didn't matter where he went for lunch. There would be memories of her everywhere he went. Every moment he had ever spent with her had been in the historical area. There wasn't an inch of space around here that didn't have some kind of memory of her attached to it.

As he wandered around the crowded streets trying to find a place to sit, he began to wonder if he could continue working in Colonial Williamsburg. He had come here in the first place to get a fresh start after his divorce. It had worked well at first, but now, with reminders of the love of his life everywhere, it was hard to imagine having the emotional strength to stay.

Lost and alone, Gregory found himself walking toward the spot where he and Rebekah always sat for lunch after all. Weary and grief-stricken, he sat down on the ground. He leaned against the tree and closed his eyes. Picturing Rebekah's sweet face, he said another silent prayer for her.

Take care of her, God. Bring her home to You. Please. End her suffering.

Gregory opened his eyes. He felt sick to his stomach but opened his lunch bag anyway. At least he could take comfort that he would be the one left behind to suffer, and not her.

He took his time eating, not tasting, his sandwich. When he was done, he got up and started walking, zombie-like, back toward the shop. He briefly considered calling in sick for the rest of the day, but then decided against it. He wasn't scheduled to work the next day, so he figured he would just power through the rest of today. Tomorrow, he would probably spend the day in bed.

He sighed heavily.

So I'll get one day of bereavement and then have to get right back to work.

The idea was exhausting.

"Hey, man, you okay?" came a voice from just in front of him.

Gregory stopped short, startled out of his trance. He'd been so out of it, he hadn't even seen Orlando approach.

"Oh, hey. Sorry," Gregory mumbled. "Yeah, I'm okay."

"The hell you are," Orlando said, looking concerned.

"Rebekah," he began cautiously, unsure if he could get the words out without breaking down. "It's ... We think it's her time. She's ready to go."

"Oh, wow," Orlando said sadly.

"She felt a strong urge to return to the river this morning."

"That must be where she died?"

"Yeah. Going back there, it's just something she knew she was supposed to do. And I, well, I don't think she's coming back. W—we said our goodbyes this morning."

"Oh, man. I'm sorry. I'm so sorry," Orlando said.

It helped to have someone to talk to about what was happening. Gregory was grateful that Orlando had dragged the truth out of him that night at the bar. It was too damned hard to hide his grief right now, and with Orlando, he didn't have to.

"It's the right thing," Gregory said. "It's for the best."

"That doesn't mean it doesn't hurt like hell."

Gregory swallowed hard.

"I hope she finds peace," Orlando said gently. "And I hope you do, too."

"Thanks."

"Is there anything I can do?"

"I don't think so. Thanks, man."

"You just let me know. Anything you need. It's my job to take care of you."

Gregory shot him a quizzical look, and Orlando smiled.

"Rebekah made me swear I'd take care of you if she ever made it to the other side."

"Really?"

"Oh, yeah," Orlando said with a gentle laugh.

"She's so sweet," Gregory said fondly. "I'm gonna miss her."

Orlando's words were good to hear. Rebekah had spent so much of her existence being invisible. It was important to Gregory that she wouldn't be forgotten.

Orlando clapped him on the back.

"I know how much you love her. I know how much this hurts. But you helped her find peace. Don't ever forget that. She's gonna finally be free because of you." He looked Gregory in the eye. "Rebekah's gonna be okay. Now you gotta make sure you are, too. Take it easy, man."

"I'll try," Gregory said weakly. "I'll try."

23

As a spirit, Rebekah could travel easily to the exact spot where Nathaniel had drowned. When she was alive, the trip had taken hours by horseback. Now she could float there in a matter of seconds. She slowed down when she got closer to where her brother had died. She walked at a normal pace once she got there because she was visible and needed to keep up appearances in case anyone saw her.

A deep sense of dread overwhelmed her. She had hated coming here in the past. Hated the way it made her feel and how it threw her into that familiar spiral of depression. She walked to the spot on the grass where she had set up the picnic for herself and her brother all those years ago. It was crazy that, after all this time, the area looked mostly the same as it had in 1762. It was in a rather remote spot and not really suitable for building much of anything. A few people walked along the edge of the water in the distance, and a young man in his twenties sat under a tree. Fortunately, they were all out of earshot, leaving Rebekah to grieve in private.

She wasn't entirely sure why she had been compelled to

return here or what she was supposed to do. She looked out at the water and simply let her emotions overtake her. The horrific memories crashed over her, much more vividly now as she stood in the exact spot where the tragedy had occurred. Overwhelmed, she broke down in sobs.

The Weeping Woman until the bitter end.

She wept for her lost little brother. She wept for losing Gregory.

And she cried, Rebekah suddenly realized, for herself.

Rebekah thought of the young woman she was that day. A loving sister who wanted nothing more than to take her brother on an outing that would make him happy. A frightened young woman who had made a terrible, irreparable mistake. That girl was terrified. Desperate. Grief-stricken. Alone. It was hard to feel hate and contempt for that young girl. All these years she had told herself she was horrible. Evil. Unworthy of love and of God's mercy. Rebekah knew that, had the tragedy happened to anyone else, she would have had tremendous empathy for the poor soul. She would have gently assured that young woman that it was just a terrible, tragic accident.

She closed her eyes and at last whispered the words, "It was an accident."

For the first time, she believed it. She was still for a few moments, listening to the sounds of the birds, the wind rippling through the trees, and the gentle lapping of the water. She felt calm and peaceful and light as the crushing weight of guilt and shame began to lift. In tune with nature and with the Earth and all its inhabitants, as well as with those who existed beyond the earthly realm.

Softly, she began to sing the lullaby she had made up for Nathaniel.

"Hush sweet little boy, close your eyes.You must get rest 'fore morning is nigh. Hush silly boy, 'tis no time to laugh."

Rebekah laughed gently as she sang that part, remembering how Nathaniel loved to giggle when the song told him not to.

"There'll be time for that when night is past."

"I like the way you sing," said a male voice.

Rebekah's eyes flew open. She was startled to see the young man who had been sitting under the tree in the distance now standing a few feet in front of her. He had brown hair and light brown eyes and was clad in blue jeans and a T-shirt.

"But then again, I always did love that song," the young man said. Then he began to sing,

"Hush now, silly boy, and get some sleep.Soon enough, the sun shall creep, and you'll have time to play, and sing and laugh all day."

Rebekah stared at the young man. "N—Nathaniel?"

He grinned. "That's me. Thought it might be a lil' creepy to show up as a well-spoken three-year-old, so I thought I'd appear looking closer to your age. Well, you know, your age when you died, anyway."

Stunned, Rebekah looked into the young man's eyes. Those playful, familiar, sweet brown eyes. She couldn't move. She couldn't speak. It was really him. *Nathaniel.* Her precious little brother was standing right before her. The urge to reach out and pull him close to her was even stronger than it had ever been with Gregory. She ached to feel her brother in her arms and hold him tight.

Nathaniel smiled fondly at her. "I forgive you, Rebekah. Of *course* I do. I wasn't allowed to come and tell you that until you forgave yourself. That's just how it works."

Overwhelmed with love, relief, and remorse, Rebekah

struggled to find her voice. "Oh, Nathaniel. I'm sorry. I'm so sorry!"

"I know you are," Nathaniel said gently. "I never blamed you for what happened, big sister. I know you love me. It was horrible, and nobody suffered more over it than you did. Not even Mama and Papa."

What a relief it was to hear Nathaniel's sweet words of forgiveness. She gazed adoringly at her brother. How handsome he was. He looked healthy and happy and perfect, just like Gregory had said.

"I forgive you," Nathaniel said firmly. "And now I want you to say it to yourself."

Hesitating only a moment, Rebekah said, "I forgive myself."

And she did. For the first time, she gave herself the gift of forgiveness. She finally felt free. Rebekah laughed with the relief of letting go of the past and from the sheer joy of seeing Nathaniel again.

"It's about time!" Nathaniel exclaimed, laughing with her. "I'm sorry you spent so much time worrying about me, Rebekah. I'm fine. I've always been perfectly fine. After the accident, I went to Heaven for a while. After that, I was born again and kind of started over."

"You did? You came back and lived all over again?"

"Yeah," he said. "I had another mom and dad and two brothers, but believe me, you and Martha and Mama and Papa are every bit as much my family as my second family is. That's the thing about love and family; it's not possible to have too much of it."

"How wonderful," Rebekah said, her heart healing as Nathanial reassured her.

"I lived a lot longer the second time."

"How old were you when you died the second time?"

"Eighty-two," Nathaniel said with a grin.

"Oh my goodness! I can't imagine you as an old man."

"I know, right? Weird," he chuckled. "Had kids and grandkids and all that. It's kind of funny to think that the whole time I was alive the second time, I didn't remember you or the rest of the family. But when you die and you go to Heaven, you remember. Your heart remembers. You're reunited with anybody and everybody you ever loved. Parents, grandparents, friends, pets. You get to be with them all."

"That's so lovely," Rebekah said.

"So," Nathaniel said cautiously. "That's how it works. When you don't live long enough to do everything you're supposed to do and learn everything you're supposed to learn, you go back and live again. Babies, miscarriages, anybody who died before their time gets another chance. Even, you know, suicides ..."

"What are you saying?"

"You gotta go back, Rebekah," he told her. "You gotta go back and start over. Don't think of it as punishment for killing yourself. It's not like that. It's more like, well, people who take their own lives usually had a rough time in life, and this gives them a chance to try again."

Rebekah's eyes grew wide. "You mean I'm going to be born all over again?"

Nathaniel nodded.

She stared at him for a moment, letting the truth sink in. Then Nathaniel grinned.

"Well, at least that's the way it would normally work. But enough people grieved for you when you died the first time. It wouldn't be fair to make Gregory go through that."

"Gregory," Rebekah said, picturing his sweet, loving brown eyes.

"He loves you so much, Rebekah. I don't just know it. I can *feel* it," Nathaniel said, placing his hand near his heart. "He's that handsome man come to sweep you off your feet you always dreamed of."

He laughed happily, and she joined in.

"Yes, he certainly is."

"I can also feel how much you love him. It just wouldn't be right to tear you guys apart. So, instead of being born all over again, you're allowed to come back just like you are now."

"Now?" Rebekah asked, incredulous.

Nathaniel chuckled. "Yes, *now*. Hadn't you noticed, big sister? You're breathing."

She gasped. Sure enough, she drew in an actual breath.

She was suddenly light-headed from the shock of breathing and the realization she had a physical body again. She staggered, and Nathaniel reached out to steady her.

Nathaniel was touching her.

He chuckled again, his eyes sparkling with love and warmth. "And oh yeah. I'm solid, too. Just for now, on this occasion, so I can hug you."

Nathaniel tenderly pulled her into his arms and held her close. Rebekah threw her arms around her baby brother and began to sob deeply.

The Weeping Woman still weeps, but now she weeps for joy.

Rebekah cried and cried as she held on to Nathaniel for dear life. After grieving for him for two hundred and fifty years, she couldn't believe she was here with her brother and holding him close.

"It's all right, it's okay," Nathaniel soothed, gently rubbing her back and letting her cry for as long as she needed to. It took quite some time for her to settle down, but he didn't seem to mind. Nathaniel held her patiently as she sobbed. In this beautiful, perfect moment, Rebekah could feel the love Nathaniel had for her. It radiated from him—pure, sweet love. It felt like a small taste of what Heaven might be like.

Eventually, Rebekah began to calm. She pulled back from her brother's warm embrace so she could wipe her eyes.

"You all right?" Nathaniel asked.

"Yes. I'm just overwhelmed, but in the most wonderful way. So I'm ... I'm going to just ... *live* ... now?"

"Yes. It won't be easy," he gently warned. "All you have right now are the clothes on your back. You're starting life with no living parents or siblings. But it's gonna be okay. Gregory and his family and the wonderful new friends you're gonna make will be all the family you need to get through life this time."

"Gregory," Rebekah said, fresh tears spilling all over again.

I'm going to spend the rest of my life with Gregory.

Nathaniel smiled, placing his hand over his heart again. He glanced out at the water, and then he turned back to her.

"Rebekah. I need you to finally lay this burden down."

"I'll try," she whispered, her voice shaky. Even now, with Nathaniel standing before her, the memory of his death still grieved her.

"You are worthy of love. Not because Gregory loves you. Not because I love you. But because you simply *are worthy*. Do you understand?"

Rebekah nodded tentatively.

"Loving yourself is the most important step toward loving others," he told her. She nodded again. "Oh, and you know that silly thing where people think dead loved ones show them items like coins and butterflies and stuff as messages?"

"Yes?"

Nathaniel grinned. "It's true."

"So, the butterflies were from you?"

"Yeah. I was trying to tell you I was okay and not to worry."

Rebekah put a hand over her heart. "I'm so glad you're all right. I love you so much."

"I love you, too, big sister." Nathaniel glanced skyward and then back at her. "Next time, we'll meet at my place."

Rebekah's eyes filled with tears. "I'll miss you 'til then."

"I know," he said gently. "But I'm always with you."

With that, Nathaniel flexed his fingers and a butterfly flitted past. Rebekah smiled as she wiped her tears.

"Oh, and before I go, I have a message for your friend, Orlando."

"You do? Oh! Is it from his—"

"Yep. From his mother." Nathaniel gave her the message, and she committed it to memory. "He'll know what it means. Just be sure to tell him."

"I will. I promise," she said, her heart filling with renewed joy just thinking of how much it would mean to Orlando to hear from his mother after all this time.

"I have to go now, Rebekah."

"Wait!" Rebekah said, panic suddenly setting in. "What do I do now that I'm alive?"

"Everything's gonna be just fine. Go and find Gregory. That's all you need to do."

"B—but I'm miles and miles away from where he is. I don't think I can get back to Colonial Williamsburg by the time they close. Gregory will have left—"

"It's okay," Nathaniel said. "You trust me, right?"

"Of course I do."

"Okay, then. Just start walking. Toward the historical district."

Rebekah's brow furrowed, knowing that walking back would mean walking along a major highway. The idea was rather terrifying.

"Trust me," he said. "Just start walking."

"Okay. I will."

"'Til we meet again, sweet sister. Go. Make it a great life."

Nathaniel grinned at her and then vanished.

"I will," she whispered.

~

REBEKAH BEGAN the hike toward Colonial Williamsburg. For so long, she'd had no reason to be afraid because nothing could cause her any physical harm. Now she felt fragile and vulnerable. Nathaniel had promised she would be all right, and of course she trusted him. But walking alone on Route 31, a busy highway with cars zooming past her, was terrifying. Sounds of roaring engines and horns honking, as well as the smell of exhaust and fuel, made her head spin.

She drew in a deep breath, and that, itself, took some getting used to. It helped, though. Breathing in and out steadily calmed her. She reminded herself that once she got through this scary part, she would be with Gregory.

Euphoria coursed through her veins just thinking about it.

Soon, I'll be in Gregory's arms. I'll be able to hold him close.

The idea was almost too wonderful to be true.

A huge truck barreled down the road close enough to blow wind through her skirt. She swallowed hard, her body quaking with fear. Everything was so new and big to her.

Just as she felt panic start to overtake her, a car pulled over to the side of the road in front of her.

A police car.

A dark-skinned officer with warm brown eyes stepped out of the vehicle.

"Ma'am? Are you all right?"

Rebekah smiled with relief.

It only took about ten minutes for the officer to drive Rebekah over to the Colonial Williamsburg Visitor Center. Thankfully, she had been able to come up with a plausible tale to explain why she had been walking down a highway all alone. She told the officer she'd taken part in a reenactment at Jamestown, which explained her old-fashioned clothing. The fib was that she was to call a friend for a ride at the end of the day, but she had accidentally left her purse with her cell phone in the car after she'd been dropped off in the morning.

Riding in the police car was an adventure to be sure. How strange it was to be traveling so fast! Frightened, Rebekah found herself tightly holding on to the car door handle. The officer must have thought her mad.

"You sure you'll be all right here?" The police officer asked as he pulled up to the front of the Visitor Center.

"Oh, yes. My boyfriend works here. He'll take care of me. Thank you. Thank you very much!"

"You're very welcome," the man said with a smile. "Take care now."

"You too," Rebekah chirped happily. How wonderful it was to have real human contact without worrying about scaring people. She could just be herself again.

She raced to the Visitor Center. It amused her that the automatic doors opened for her after sensing her presence. Of course, she'd been inside the Visitor Center thousands of times, but it felt so strange to have to use the door to get in. She realized she would need to remember that. No more walking through doors and walls. If she tried that now, she might get hurt. The thought made her laugh.

Rebekah ran the whole way to Hay's Cabinetmaker's Shop. It was just past 5pm, and the historical buildings were closing. She had to catch Gregory before he left for the day, lest she be stranded overnight with no way to reach him. He had a cell phone of course, but she didn't know the number. She never dreamed she would need it.

Her heart soared when she saw Gregory walking out of the back door of the shop and locking it behind him.

"Gregory!" she cried, and he whirled around to see her running toward him.

She had thought about playing it cool and not telling him straight away that she was alive. It would have been fun to see if he figured it out, but she was far too excited and was gasping for breath. The sooner she explained to him what had happened, the sooner she could grab onto him and never let go.

"Rebekah," he said, his eyes full of relief. "I guess I shouldn't be happy to see you, but I can't help it."

Gregory's eyes grew wide. "Y—y—you're out of breath. How can you be *out of breath*?"

He looked bewildered and even a bit afraid. It reminded Rebekah of the day she first appeared to him as a ghost.

"Oh, Gregory, the most wonderful thing has happened!" she cried. "I went to the river like I knew I was supposed to. I was there for a while and thought about everything. I finally made peace with the tragedy, and I said the words out loud."

He stared at her for a moment, unable to speak. He looked her up and down, trying to figure out what in blazes was going on. "W—what ... what words?"

"It was an accident," she said, feeling the sense of relief all over again. "I said out loud that it was an accident. I told my brother how sorry I was, and I even sang for him. You know, that special lullaby I made up just for him?"

Gregory nodded, still looking dazed.

"I sang it for him, and then my brother came to me. He came to see me. I actually got to see Nathaniel!" Rebekah cried out joyously.

That bit of information managed to snap him out of his shock.

"You did? Oh, Rebekah, that's wonderful. What did he say?"

"He said he forgave me. He wasn't a little boy anymore. He appeared to me looking about my age, and he was healthy and beautiful and perfect," Rebekah gushed. "He told me he never really blamed me in the first place for what happened."

She began to cry as she spoke about her brother, shedding sweet tears of joy and relief.

"Look," she exclaimed, wiping her eyes. "Tears. Real tears."

Gregory's eyes grew wider. "Rebekah, what in the world is going on with you?"

"Nathaniel told me that because of everything that happened before ... because I took my own life, I'm supposed to try again. Live all over again and do everything I was supposed to do the first time. That's what he did. He started all over again as a baby and had a new mother and father and a whole new life," she said, her words coming out in a rush. Gregory furrowed his brow and nodded, trying to keep up with what she was saying. "And because I died so young, that's what I was supposed to do. Normally, I would be reborn and start all over again. But instead ...

because of you ... because of our love ... I get to come back now."

Rebekah watched his face as the words sank in.

Trembling and with fresh tears in her eyes, she said, "Gregory, I'm alive."

He stared at her.

"No ... it can't be. It can't be ... possible," he said.

Rebekah saw the fear in Gregory's eyes. As if he were afraid to hope.

"It ... it can't be ..." he repeated. Shaking, he reached out his hand to press his fingers to her mouth.

And touched her lips.

Gregory gasped when he made contact with her, feeling warmth instead of cold. Rebekah laughed happily.

"You're alive. You're really alive!" he cried, touching the rest of her face.

"Yes, I really am."

He threw his arms around her, lifting her slightly off the ground. He held on as if he would never let her go.

"Gregory," was all she could say as she reveled in the healing power of his touch. It had been achingly long since she had been touched, and today she had held and been physically cherished by two of the people she loved the most. She had never known such joy was possible.

"Rebekah, my sweet Rebekah," he said as he touched her as much as he could. He rubbed her back, stroked her hair, and nuzzled her cheek.

I can physically feel his love. It was so pure, so powerful, that it really did transcend the physical.

Gregory pulled back slightly. Caressing her cheek, he asked, "Are you all right? Do you feel all right?"

"Yes, I'm fine. I feel a little weak, and I'm still getting used to walking around and being like this, but I'm fine."

"My God, how did you get back here from the river?"

"I walked down Route 31."

He looked alarmed.

"It's okay. I didn't get far before a police officer saw me and gave me a ride back here."

"Oh," he said, letting out a breath of relief. "Thank God I was still here."

"I know. I wasn't looking forward to spending the night here all by myself. I figure I've done that enough over the years."

Eyes filled with wonder, Gregory ran his fingers through her hair. It was a delicious feeling, relaxing and exciting all at once. She wondered if she would ever get used to the thrill of being touched by the man she loved. She rather hoped not.

He gazed down at her, his dark brown eyes full of such passion and intensity that it made her knees go weaker than they already were.

"Rebekah," he said in a sensual, husky voice. "Have you ever been kissed?"

"No," she whispered.

"May I have the honor?" he asked, the intensity in his gaze deepening.

"Of course," she replied, gazing up at him with delicious anticipation.

Fierce desire burned in his eyes, and she could feel how desperately he wanted to kiss her. And yet, he took his time. A first kiss was a big deal, and it melted her heart to see how much he understood that.

He threaded his fingers through her hair and gazed intently into her eyes.

"Rebekah," was all he said. It was all he needed to say.

Gregory dipped his head and pressed his lips to hers.

An explosion of desire and love and sweetness erupted within her. She wrapped her arms around him as his tender kiss deepened, enveloping her. Her entire body tingled with passion and love as she experienced the best reminder yet that she was well and truly alive.

Rebekah's knees weakened at Gregory's delicious, sensuous kiss. He must have sensed it, because his strong arms tightened around her. Supporting her. Protecting her. Loving her.

When their lips finally parted, she gazed up into those soulful brown eyes with those lovely, long eyelashes.

"I love you," she said.

"I love you too," Gregory said, gently caressing her cheek.

They spent a moment simply enjoying being wrapped in each other's arms. Eventually, Rebekah spoke.

"What do we do now?" she asked.

"I take you home with me. And from now on, it's not just my home. It's *ours*."

Gregory slipped his arm around her waist and guided her toward the parking lot.

24

How is this possible? How can this actually be possible? The thought echoed over and over in Gregory's mind. A part of him worried it might all be a dream. That he might wake up tomorrow morning feeling empty and bereft with the realization that Rebekah had crossed over and left him behind.

But she hadn't crossed over.

Gregory was walking with his arm wrapped around her waist. He was *touching* her. He had *kissed* her. He was taking her home with him.

He squeezed her excitedly and she squeezed him back.

I will never, ever take touching her for granted.

As they neared the Visitor Center parking lot, a butterfly flitted past them.

Rebekah gasped.

"Are you all right?" Gregory asked her.

"Yes," she said softly. "The butterfly. That's a sign from Nathaniel. Remember how I told you I've seen butterflies at the strangest times, and I always wondered if they were from him? They were. He told me so."

"Wow. It must have been so wonderful to see him again."

"It was," she said happily.

Gregory had never seen Rebekah look so joyful. At last, the depressed look in her eyes was gone.

She wobbled, unsteady on her feet.

"You sure you're all right?"

"Yes, I'm just fine. I'd forgotten how intense the heat is in Virginia in August," she proclaimed, fanning her face. "But I don't mind. It's good to feel something. *Anything*."

"I feel like I should be carrying you after everything you've been through," Gregory said.

Rebekah laughed. "That won't be necessary."

"I don't know. I think it is."

With that, he scooped her off her feet and into his arms. She cried out in surprise, making several tourists in the parking lot turn to look. They probably thought he was kidnapping her.

She giggled joyously and threw her arms around his neck. Gregory heard some chuckles from the nearby tourists now that it was clear she was his willing victim.

"It's funny," she said, gazing adoringly into his eyes. "Nathaniel knew all about you."

"Yeah?"

"He said he knew how much we loved each other, and he said I finally found the handsome man I always dreamed of to come sweep me off my feet." She giggled again, kicking her feet in the air. Gregory was more than happy to play the part of the handsome prince for her.

"So little brother approves of me for his big sister, does he?"

Rebekah smiled. "He sure does."

I'm glad you're at peace, Nathaniel. And I'll take good care of your big sister. I swear to it.

Gregory grinned at her, kissed her, and then gently set her back on her feet so he could open the car door for her. She sat down inside the car and he closed the door after her.

He sat behind the wheel for a moment, the day's events finally catching up with him. Gregory stared straight ahead, feeling Rebekah's eyes on him. He looked down at his lap, fighting tears.

"Are you all right?" she asked softly.

"I thought ... All day today, I thought when I got back in my car in the evening, I'd be leaving you behind forever. When we said goodbye at the bridge, I thought that was it."

"I know. I thought that too."

Not wanting her to see the tears in his eyes, Gregory kept his head down when he turned toward her to pull her into his arms.

"I thought you were gone," he said in a shaky voice as he held her.

"I know," she soothed. "I know. But I'm not, darling. I'm here."

They held each other close. After a moment, he pulled back, wiping his eyes.

"Okay," he said with a laugh. "I'm okay, now. I promise."

"Good," Rebekah said, gently touching his cheek.

"You've been trapped in this place long enough. Let's get you out of here," he said, reaching across her to put on her seatbelt for her. "I only wish I lived a bit further away for your sake."

"I don't care. I just want to go home with you."

Gregory drove out of the parking lot and headed toward his apartment building.

"Oh my goodness," she said, her voice filled with wonder

after they had driven for a few minutes. Gregory glanced over at her to see her eyes wide as she took in all the restaurants, shops, gas stations, and office buildings.

"What?"

"Just everything. Everything is different from what I'm used to. I haven't been away from the Colonial Williamsburg area ... well ... *ever*. When I was alive, our family never traveled too far from here, and since I died, I haven't been able to go more than a few miles away. Everything around here is so big and so different."

"I hope it's not too overwhelming for you."

"It is overwhelming, but in the most wonderful way. Of course I know about places like this. I've heard of McDonald's and Burger King and Starbucks and all of that. I know about them from TV commercials and from people's conversations, but it's so exciting to actually see it all!"

He grinned, getting caught up in her excitement.

"Gregory, you have to take me to McDonald's sometime," she chirped.

He laughed. "It's a date. I promise."

Rebekah got quiet for a while.

"What are you thinking about, sweet girl?"

"I was wondering if you still wanted to get married now that it's actually possible."

His heart leapt in his chest. There was so much he hadn't considered yet.

"My God, Rebekah. We can get *married*."

"Yes, we can," she said.

"Rebekah, not only am I gonna marry you, but I'm gonna give you the prettiest, girliest wedding you ever saw."

She laughed and then turned to look at him. "You know none of that really matters, right? All that matters is that we're together."

"Yeah. I know that. But I'm still gonna do it."

She got quiet again.

"You're already thinking about your wedding gown, aren't you?"

Rebekah burst into laughter. "Yes! You know me so well."

"Yeah, I sure do."

Gregory frowned as he realized there was something he hadn't considered.

"I definitely want to marry you, Rebekah, but it might take a while. In the eyes of the law, you don't even exist, so right now there's no way to make our marriage legal. But don't you worry. We'll get it all sorted out. I'm sure there's some way to get a paper trail started so we can get you some legal identification and stuff like that."

"You're right. I hadn't thought about any of that. It's just as well, I suppose."

"Why do you say that?"

"Well, this will give your family some time to get used to the idea of you and me. I would hate for them to think I was a homewrecker if we married so soon after your divorce."

"I'm sure they wouldn't think that," Gregory reassured her. "My family's gonna love you. I always said if they ever got the chance to see us together, they would understand why we were perfect together."

"And then there's Vanessa."

"What about her?"

"I'm rather glad we're not going to marry right away. For her sake. I imagine it might be painful for her to know you were married again not long after divorcing her."

"You're right. I hadn't thought about that. You're so sweet to think of her feelings, Rebekah."

Gregory pulled into the parking lot of his apartment building.

"This is it," he said.

"Wow, it's enormous," she exclaimed, looking up at the tall structure.

"I mean, this is the entire apartment building. I just live in one of the apartment units."

Rebekah gave him a wry look. "I'm aware of that, darling. I wasn't born yesterday. Not even close."

He laughed. "Sorry. It's just hard to be sure what you know and what you don't."

"I know. It's okay."

Gregory got out of the car and walked to the other side to help her out. He was impressed that she'd already gotten her seatbelt off by herself. He couldn't imagine how lost he would be feeling if he were in her shoes right now, and he knew he had to make her feel comfortable with living in the modern world without talking down to her. After all, she was quite intelligent and had experienced more time on Earth than he ever would. He was sure Rebekah had a thing or two to teach him as well.

His apartment was on the second floor, and he chose to take the stairs rather than the elevator. One new experience at a time, he figured.

"I'm warning you. It's not much," Gregory said as he unlocked the door.

"Oh, it's beautiful," Rebekah exclaimed when she got her first glimpse of the modest apartment. He watched her eyes as she surveyed the small kitchen with all the modern appliances, and then the living room with the fluffy beige couch, coffee table, and television. It was pretty standard stuff, but seeing it all through her eyes made him appreciate everything he had.

Rebekah smiled as she walked directly over to his favorite spot in the apartment. The piano.

"I can't wait to hear you play this," she said.

"And I can't wait to have you sing with me."

"It's lovely. Did you make this?" she asked as she lovingly ran her fingers over the wooden piano.

"Oh, no. I don't think I could make anything that exquisite. I did spend a fortune on it, I don't mind telling you."

"Considering how much music means to you, I'm sure it was worth every penny."

Gregory felt a lump in his throat. Rebekah understood. She always understood. He gave her a tour of the rest of the apartment, and he could have sworn she blushed when he showed her the bedroom. It was utterly endearing, and he looked forward to many more opportunities to make her blush.

"Are you hungry?" he asked as they made their way back to the kitchen.

"Yes, I rather am. I— Gregory! You haven't eaten yet!"

He chuckled. "I'm fine, Rebekah. I do need to eat soon, but I'm fine. What do you want for dinner?"

"Do you know what I've always wanted to try? A cheeseburger. Better yet, a bacon cheeseburger."

"Sounds good to me. And you also gotta try french fries."

"Yes! A burger and fries. What could be more modern than that?"

He laughed, loving her enthusiasm. "Perfect. I'll get some food delivered. I promise I'll take you out to McDonald's and other places, but I don't want to throw too many new things at you all at once."

Gregory called a local restaurant to order the food, all the while watching Rebekah and smiling as she explored the apartment. She stood right near an air conditioning vent, breathing in the cool air, and he thought of how strange it must feel to be cool and comfortable inside on a hot summer day. He shook his head, remembering Rebekah's story of how they had cooked outside in the middle of the summer.

To say she enjoyed her dinner would be an understatement. She savored every bite, and he savored every moment watching her.

"Would it be all right if I took a bath before bed?" she asked shyly. "In my day, we didn't wash as much as you all do now."

"Of course. I don't have a bathtub, though. Only a shower. I'll show you how it works."

Gregory grabbed a new toothbrush from a pack in the linen closet and ushered her into the bathroom adjoining his bedroom. He showed her how to brush her teeth with toothpaste, and then he taught her how to turn on the warm and cold water in the shower.

"I'm sorry I don't have any girl clothes for you to wear, but tomorrow I'll take you shopping, and we can get you some stuff. You can wear this tonight." He handed her one of his button-down shirts, as well as a pair of cotton shorts for underneath.

"Thank you," she said with a smile.

"I'll wash your dress and underthings, too, so you can wear them tomorrow when we go out."

Rebekah nodded, and he left her alone in the bathroom to shower.

Gregory's eyes nearly popped out of his head when she emerged from the bathroom after showering. The shirt he'd given her clung to her small yet perfect breasts, and it showed off her lovely legs.

She wrapped her arms around her chest for a moment, avoiding his gaze. Gregory knew he shouldn't stare but he couldn't stop himself. Poor, sweet Rebecca. She must be feeling so vulnerable. In her day, a woman would never have shown that much skin to anyone, especially not to a man who wasn't her husband.

Slowly, she lowered her arms. Looking down at his shirt hanging loosely off her body, she said self-consciously, "I must look ridiculous in this."

"Are you kidding? You look sexy as hell right now," he blurted out.

Rebekah looked at him in surprise. After meeting his gaze, she understood he was serious.

"No one's ever called me sexy before," she said shyly.

"Get used to it, because I'm gonna be saying it a lot."

He stared at Rebekah, knowing he was going to have to control his suddenly raging libido. Not only was she a virgin, she had only been alive again for a few hours. He needed to take his time with her and make her as comfortable as possible during this crazy transition from death back into life.

Gregory got up from the bed and went over to her, hoping she wouldn't notice his erection.

"Rebekah," he said, gazing down at her admiringly. "I've been thinking about the sleeping arrangements, and we can do whatever you want. You can sleep in the bed with me of course, but if you don't want to, I'll be happy to sleep on the couch, and you can have the bed."

She glanced at Gregory's double bed, and then back at him. "I think I'd really like to be in bed with you. You know, j —j—just to sleep."

There was that adorable blush again.

"Of course, of course," he said gently. "As long as you're comfortable with it, that's what we'll do. I usually sleep in just my underwear, but I'll put on some sweatpants and a T-shirt tonight."

Rebekah nodded thoughtfully. "Well, how about just the pants? I rather like the idea of cuddling up against your bare skin."

"That does sound nice."

After Gregory washed up and brushed his teeth, he emerged from the bathroom wearing only sweatpants. Rebekah eyed his chest appreciatively.

"Now who looks sexy as hell?" she said, blushing but still bravely looking him in the eye.

Gregory grinned at her. The flash of desire in her eyes warmed him all over. He got into bed and she climbed in next to him. He turned on his side, wanting to get a good look at her before he turned out the light. He could hardly believe she was here, filling the spot in the bed that had felt cold and lonely since they met.

"How are you feeling?" he asked.

"Happier than I ever knew was possible."

"Me too."

Gregory turned out the light on his nightstand, and Rebekah slid over and nestled close to him. She rested her head on his bare chest. He wrapped his arms around her, wanting to make sure she felt safe and warm and oh, so loved.

25

Rebekah was alive and happy and in love, and the next day had felt like an adventure. Gregory had taken her grocery and clothes shopping. He'd bought her beautiful dresses and other outfits, and she even got measured by a saleswoman for the right size bra. It was a bit awkward at first, but wearing a lovely, lacy bra made her feel like a modern woman. One of her favorite new discoveries of the day was Coca-Cola. Like bacon cheeseburgers, she had always wanted to try it. Gregory had laughed when she declared her love for the sweet, fizzy drink.

Every moment with Gregory felt like a precious gift. Laughing and talking with him, being able to kiss him and hold him anytime she wished. It was all simply magical. He made her transition back to life as smooth as possible. He knew how to show her new things without ever making her feel stupid. He provided assistance and advice when she needed it, but he also seemed to know when to step back and let her try things for herself. He protected her without making her feel helpless, and that meant a great deal to her.

Gregory had to return to work the next day. She assured

him she would be fine by herself in the apartment. He showed her how to use the Internet, so she'd spent the entire first day alone reading up on the latest news, learning how to cook and clean with modern appliances, as well as how to cook and care for a person who was diabetic. Rebekah had always loved to read and learn, and she found it incredibly exciting that she could learn about any topic she wished at the touch of a button.

Though she knew, in theory, about how modern cooking worked, it was an odd feeling to be able to cook anything without using fire. Cooking macaroni and cheese on the stovetop for lunch had been a learning experience. Many times throughout the day she'd had to remind herself that she could touch things now. For centuries, she'd dealt with the limitations of being a ghost. Now, it was a thrill to be able to lift a cup of hot tea to her lips. She was still getting used to being among the living.

The doorbell rang once while she was home alone, and it frightened her. She was wary about answering the door to a stranger. Looking through the peephole, she saw it was a delivery man. Hesitantly, she opened the door just a crack.

The man smiled. "Delivery for Ms. Jennings?"

"For me?" she asked, astonished.

The man chuckled. "Yeah, I guess so. Here you go."

He held the package up for her, and she opened the door just wide enough to accept it.

"Thank you."

"You're very welcome, ma'am. Have a good day now."

"You too."

Rebekah closed the door, locked it, then inspected the package. She set the box down on the kitchen table and opened it. Inside was tissue paper with a card on top. It read: *To the most beautiful woman alive.*

She unwrapped the paper to find lovely fresh flowers. Lilacs, fragrant and colorful; the most thoughtful gift she'd ever received. Rebekah freed them from the box and clutched them to her chest.

And she began to weep.

She collapsed onto one of the kitchen chairs, holding the flowers close and sobbing with relief. So much had happened so fast, and she was still processing it all. She was alive. Gregory loved her. Nathaniel was happy and at peace.

Her long nightmare was over.

After she'd wiped her eyes and composed herself, Rebekah got up and put the lilacs into a glass with water. Then she went into the living room and caught sight of herself in the mirror. Her eyes were red from crying, but other than that, she looked okay in her pretty new dress.

Rebekah stared at her reflection, truly seeing herself for the first time in a long time. She looked into her own eyes and saw an imperfect person. One who had made mistakes. And yet, she also saw a person who did her best, gave love freely, and wanted to do good in the world. She reflected on her brother's sage words about being worthy of love.

Staring in the mirror, she realized she agreed with him. Yes, she was messy and flawed and imperfect, but who wasn't? She tried her best, and that really was good enough.

I will make it a good life, Nathaniel. I promise.

∽

"Have a good day, sweetheart," Gregory said as he prepared to leave for work the next morning. "You have everything you need?"

She nodded. He had given her one of his credit cards for emergencies, and even found an old cell phone he'd hooked up for her so he could call her during the day. He'd thought of everything to keep her safe and comfortable.

"You too," she said.

Gregory put his arms around her and kissed her goodbye. When his kiss deepened and became more passionate, Rebekah's body tingled all over, and a soft moan escaped her throat. She felt her knees go weak, just as they had when he'd kissed her for the first time. She became aware of the hardness between his legs. He *wanted* her.

As if realizing he was getting carried away, Gregory broke off the kiss. He pulled back, swallowing hard. It was fascinating to watch him try to compose himself, and Rebekah could hardly believe she was the reason for his loss of control. In her first life, people had called her pretty sometimes, but no one had ever made her feel sexy the way Gregory did.

"You want to make love, don't you?" she asked, gazing into his eyes.

"Rebekah, you're the most beautiful woman in the world, living or dead. Not to mention the most desirable. *Of course* I want to make love to you," he told her. Then he smiled and gently brushed her hair behind her ear. "But I'll understand if you want to wait until we're married. You are from a different time and all."

She looked into those sweet brown eyes, somehow falling even more in love with him. He was so thoughtful and patient, forever putting her needs above his own.

"Yes. I am from a different time. And I've waited long enough, don't you think?"

Gregory's eyes flashed with excitement, and yet he remained cool and calm. "What ... what are you saying?"

"I'm saying that I want nothing more than for you to make love to me," Rebekah said. She hadn't even realized that she was ready until the words came out of her mouth. And yet, she had no regrets. She *was* ready. She knew more than anyone that life was short, and that tomorrow was promised to no one.

"You're sure," he asked cautiously, his eyes practically blazing with desire. Rebekah's heart melted. She could see he was aching to have sex, but he still wanted to make sure he wasn't rushing her.

"Very sure," she said, lifting her lips to his as if to seal the deal.

"Tonight?"

"Yes."

Gregory grinned at her, then nuzzled her neck. He murmured in her ear, "How the hell am I supposed to concentrate on work all day?"

She giggled. "It'll be hard for me to wait too. But I'll see you tonight."

He kissed her again, more tenderly this time. "I'll see you tonight, my love."

Rebekah's nervousness and excitement continued through the day. She looked forward to Gregory's return from work, but she was anxious and jittery at the same time. She did her best to stay busy, but it was difficult to concentrate on reading anything on the Internet. She researched some articles on having sex for the first time, but she found they made her more nervous, so she stopped reading them. Everything she needed to know, she knew Gregory would teach her.

She took a shower in the afternoon and put on her new lacy bra and panties, as well as a new light blue dress. Then she got to work preparing him a delicious dinner. It helped a lot to have something to do besides wait.

She jumped when she heard Gregory's key in the lock in

the evening. Her heart raced and her hands trembled; she knew she needed to get ahold of herself.

Shutting the apartment door behind him, Gregory took a step back to admire her. "Rebekah, you look beautiful."

His smile was tender. He knew she was nervous. Rebekah was sure of it. But that was okay. He'd be gentle and ease her through everything. She looked into his eyes and knew she had nothing to fear.

Gregory was dashing as always in his work uniform, and she could hardly believe she now had the ability to unbutton his shirt. And she likely would soon; a notion that was both exciting and a tad frightening.

"What smells so good in here?" Gregory asked, setting down a large paper bag on the counter.

"Spaghetti and meatballs. I remember you saying it's your favorite."

"It sure is. That was so sweet of you. Thank you," he said, pulling her into his arms. He kissed her, and she felt the heat radiating from him. She had half a mind to skip dinner and head straight for the bedroom.

But that wouldn't do. Gregory needed to eat, and she was happy to feed him.

Rebekah poured him a drink of unsweetened tea with lemon and got him settled at the table.

"This ... is ... amazing," he said after taking a bite. "There's real tomatoes in here. Did you make the sauce from scratch?"

She shrugged. "Of course."

"Wow. You're incredible."

She took a few bites. The dinner had turned out quite well, and she was pleased with Gregory's reaction.

"I promise you're not always gonna be stuck here alone."

"What do you mean?"

"I've been thinking. I know we have tons of things to sort out, but you can do anything you want. I mean, if you want to stay at home, that's fine. Like when we have kids ... that is, *if* we have kids. I'm not sure if you want kids, or ..."

"You can say *when* we have kids. I definitely want to have children with you."

He nodded, his eyes lighting up.

What a good father he will be.

"So, if you wanted to stay home when we have kids, that's fine. But if you want to have a career, that's fine too. No rush to decide. There's a lot to think about. I just want you to know you have lots of options. Like once we get some paperwork on you, you can go to school if you want."

"My goodness, I'd never thought of that," she said, rather liking the idea of going to college.

"Yeah, can you imagine? After all those times sitting in on classes at the College of William and Mary, you could actually attend for real."

Rebekah chewed her bite of spaghetti thoughtfully, her mind suddenly spinning with possibilities.

"Like I said, no rush at all to make up your mind. I just want you to know, whatever you want to do, we'll make it happen."

"Right now, all I want is to have sex with you."

Gregory nearly choked on his bite of food, and Rebekah threw her head back and laughed. She hadn't been able to resist saying it, just to see what he would do.

"You all right?" she asked as he took a sip of tea.

"Yup. Just fine," he said, laughing.

They finished their meal and cleared the table in record time.

"Wait here. I'll be right back, okay?" Gregory said.

"Okay."

Rebekah watched curiously as he picked up the paper bag and headed into the bedroom. He came back to get her a few minutes later.

"Follow me," he said.

Her heart fluttered in her chest as she followed him to the bedroom.

This is it.

She drew in a deep breath, trying to steady her nerves. Gregory opened the door to the bedroom and gestured for her to go in first.

The lights were out, but Gregory had lit several candles. They bathed the room in soft, romantic light. Rebekah gasped when she saw the bed was covered in rose petals.

He shoved his hands in his pockets, giving her a rather sheepish look. "I know how much you like this kinda stuff, so I tried to, you know, make it girly for you."

Turning back to look at the room, Rebekah placed her hand over her heart. "Oh, Gregory, this is so romantic."

"Good," he breathed, sounding relieved.

"How thoughtful, Gregory. How perfect," she said, pulling him close and kissing him. He eagerly returned her kiss, and then he gently pulled her to the bed.

They sat down, side by side. She drew in a shaky breath, and he wrapped his arm around her. Her tense muscles relaxed at his touch. Resting her head on his shoulder, she let out the breath she'd been holding.

"It's okay to be nervous, sweetheart. But you don't have to worry. You're safe with me."

"I know. I just ... I don't know ... I don't know what I'm supposed to ... do."

She looked at him helplessly, feeling incredibly out of her element. She knew how sex worked, but she wasn't sure how to get started or what was expected of her.

"I'll show you what to do," he said calmly. "You touch me any way you want, and I'll touch you. We'll go slow. As we go, you tell me what feels good to you. And be sure to tell me if anything makes you feel uncomfortable."

Rebekah was comforted by his soothing voice. She trusted Gregory completely, which made the whole thing much easier on her.

Gregory kissed her again. He undid the first two buttons of his shirt, and then guided her hands to his chest to let her finish the job. She unbuttoned it the rest of the way and pulled it off him. Running her hands over the smattering of hair on his chest, she reveled in the hard, masculine feel of his body.

"Mmmm," he said approvingly. "It feels good when you touch me like that."

She rubbed his chest for a bit longer, and then she stood up from the bed. She reached out and pulled Gregory up.

"You can take off my dress now," she told him.

He reached down to grasp the hem of her dress, and he pulled it off. Her body tensed slightly as she stood there, feeling exposed. He took a step back, admiring her silky black bra and panties.

"My God, you're beautiful."

No longer feeling exposed and vulnerable, now she felt sensual. She wasn't a plain woman in a boring dress anymore. Standing there in exotic underclothes, she was the object of his desire. Her confidence building, she unbuckled Gregory's pants and let them fall to the floor. The corners of his mouth lifted as he stepped out of his pants. Clearly, he enjoyed it when she took the lead, even for a moment.

Gregory pulled her close and kissed her again, pressing the hardness of his manhood against the soft mound between her legs. She let out a moan against his lips. All this time, she had been so nervous about losing her virginity that she hadn't realized how badly she needed sexual release. Being with him felt like a new and wonderful awakening.

He cupped her breasts, making her moan all over again. His hands felt rough and yet so tender. Before Gregory, she had never been touched by a man before. The sensation was electric. The more he explored her body, the more desperate she grew for his touch. She reached behind her and unclasped her bra, then pulled it off and tossed it to the floor. Gregory touched her naked breasts. Her nipples grew hard with desire.

"Rebekah," he said, making her own name sound sensual in her ears.

Without looking down, she grasped the elastic of his underwear and pulled. He was completely naked.

"Look at me, Rebekah," he said. "I want you to look at me."

She looked into his eyes, then dropped her gaze to see his cock for the first time.

"It's okay to touch me," he gently encouraged. "But only if you want to."

Tentatively, she reached out and began to stroke him.

Gregory grunted, grabbing hold of her shoulders. "God, that feels good."

Rebekah kept going, pleased with his reaction, and proud of herself for being brazen enough to reach out and touch him. She watched his eyes as she stroked him, loving his hazy, pleased look.

He pulled her close and kissed her again. Then he slid his hand down the front of her panties, the only stitch of clothing that remained on her. Carefully, he slid two fingers up and inside her.

"Oh!" she cried with delight at the sweet invasion. Her eyes opened wide and she panted.

"It that all right? Does that feel good?"

"Yes," she breathed. "Yes, it does."

She gripped his shoulders just has he had done while she was stroking him. He slid his fingers in and out of her for a while, making her slick with arousal. Pleasurable sensations swirled inside of her. If he could make her feel this good using only his fingers, she could not begin to imagine how it would feel with his manhood inside of her. Gregory kissed her, and then scooped her up into his arms. He laid her down and slid her panties off.

Rebekah drew in a deep breath, taking in the sweet scent of the petals Gregory had scattered. She wanted to remember every detail of her first time with him. The scent of the flowers, the soft flickering of the candles, his manly scent of sawdust, the feel of his touch. It was all so beautiful.

Gregory reached over to his nightstand and pulled out a condom. She watched, fascinated, as he rolled it onto his cock. He straddled her on the bed, bending down to kiss her softly. She was grateful he was taking his time.

Gazing lovingly into her eyes, he asked, "Are you ready?"

She nodded, feeling all her muscles tighten up. She was ready, but she was afraid.

"Try to relax, my love," he said gently. "I'm afraid it might hurt more if you're tense."

Rebekah took in a few breaths and let them out, willing her body to relax. Once again. Gregory pulled back for a moment, waiting for her to be ready. Then he kissed her again.

"I love you," he whispered.

Before she had a chance to respond, he pushed himself gently but firmly inside her. She let out a cry of pain and he winced. He kissed her cheek and down her neck, remaining still inside her, giving her body a chance to adjust to the feel of him.

"You okay?" he asked.

"Yes," she whispered, the discomfort already subsiding. Her eyes spilled over with tears.

"Oh, sweetheart. I'm sorry. I didn't want to hurt you," he said, gazing into her eyes with concern.

"No. It's not that. I'm just ... emotional. I can't believe we're doing this. How is this possible?" she asked him in wonder.

Gregory smiled at her. "It's a miracle, that's all."

"Yes," Rebekah said, wiping her eyes. She wrapped her arms around his neck. "I'm all right now. I promise."

He began to move inside her, carefully watching her face.

"That feels wonderful, darling," she reassured him.

He began to slide in and out of her faster, and a soft moan escaped her lips. Her initial discomfort was quickly turning to pleasure.

Gregory Markham is making love to me.

It was a dream come true. She loved Gregory, body and soul. How glorious it was to be able to express her love physically.

His thrusts soon became quicker and more urgent. Rebekah gripped his back, loving the feel of him inside of her. He started panting heavily, and then slowed his thrusts.

Gregory surprised Rebekah by pulling out of her altogether. She didn't understand why at first. He was wearing protection, so he couldn't be worried about spilling his seed inside her. He lay next to her and slipped his fingers down between her legs.

Her body lit with fresh desire, and she finally understood.

He wants to pleasure me first.

She drew in a sharp breath, and Gregory grinned at her. He teased her opening for a bit with his fingers, softly stroking her most sensitive spot.

"Oh!" she cried, making his sexy grin widen.

"Does that feel good?" he asked in a husky voice. He clearly knew the answer, but he wanted to hear her say it.

"Yes, oh yes, it feels good. Keep doing it. Keep touching me there," she pleaded.

The sensation of bliss was indescribable. To go from feeling nothing for so long, to feeling *this* ... it was pleasure overload. Rebekah had never known anything could feel this good. She could hardly believe the sounds that came from her own mouth. They were the sensual sounds her sister had made when her new husband had made love to her. They were the sounds of ecstasy she had heard countless times on television and in movies over the years. Now it was her turn to learn firsthand what all the fuss was about. She had finally taken a lover. And what a lover he was. Handsome, strong, and tender all at once. Gregory knew instinctively how to touch her, to drive her absolutely mad with delight.

Moaning, Rebekah closed her eyes and surrendered to her lover's touch. Gregory stroked between her legs until the sweet sensation was nearly unbearably wonderful. And yet she knew, it would somehow get even better before it was over.

When she opened her eyes, she saw him watching her face as she writhed and moaned at his touch. It aroused her even more to see how much he was enjoying her reaction.

"Oh, Gregory," she barely managed to say. Ever attuned

to her needs, Gregory stroked her faster and faster until she threw her head back and cried out with release. She closed her eyes again as she reached an incredibly powerful climax that rocked her entire body.

Panting, Rebekah reveled in unfamiliar sensations of deep relaxation and utter relief. She hadn't realized how much she had needed sexual release until she finally got it.

After catching her breath, she said in the sultriest voice she could manage, "It's good to be alive."

Gregory grinned at her. Then he straddled her again, sliding into her much easier this time. Not only had her body stretched to accommodate his size, but all her womanly parts were tingly and swollen from her arousal and release. Gregory's thrusts felt utterly pleasurable now, and she could enjoy the rhythm of his lovemaking.

I'm actually doing it. I'm having sex.

Gregory began to pant again, and she loved watching his face as he made love to her. It made her happy that she could give him such pleasure using her body. Her *body*. She was a real, living woman, able to give herself to the man she loved.

As she watched him, she realized he was getting close to finishing. She wanted to assure him he could thrust as hard as he wished without causing her discomfort.

"Oh, Gregory," she said. "You feel so good inside me."

He groaned, and it thrilled her to see how much her words turned him on. His sexy eyes with those impossibly long lashes fluttered closed, and she felt his body quake as he climaxed inside of her.

Wrapping her arms around him, Rebekah felt full and happy and complete. After holding each other for a moment, Gregory pulled out of her. He disposed of the condom in the wastebasket next to the bed, then lay down beside her.

Gregory turned on his side to face her, and she smiled at him. Glancing around at the flickering candles and then back at him, she said, "Thank you for making my first time so special."

"You were amazing," he told her. Rebekah could see the relief in his eyes. He had been incredibly patient with her, and she was glad to know his needs had finally been fulfilled.

"So were you," she said, her eyes tearing up again.

"Are you okay?"

"Yes," she said, wiping her eyes. "I'm just very, very happy."

"You deserve happiness."

Rebekah thought for a moment. "I do, don't I?"

He looked surprised and pleased. He understood the significance of her words.

"Yes, you certainly do."

"I think I finally know that now. I deserve to be happy. Everyone does."

He took her in his arms and held her close.

"It's funny how they call it losing your virginity. I don't feel as if I've lost anything. I feel like I've gained a lover and a beautiful connection with you."

He stroked her hair fondly as he listened to her talk.

"Sex is such a beautiful thing," she mused. "A wonderful way to make a baby."

"The best way I know of."

Rebekah laughed. "You know what I mean."

"Yes, I do."

"If we have a baby someday, I want to name it Nathaniel."

"Okay. On one condition."

She eyed him curiously.

"Only if it's a boy."

She giggled. "Fair enough."

"If it's a girl ... I don't know. Natalie?"

Rebekah smiled. "Yes. That might work." She fell quiet for a moment. "I worry I won't be a good mother. After what happened before ... I don't have much confidence in myself when it comes to taking care of a child."

"Well, I have every confidence in you, Rebekah. And guess what? I don't know the first thing about being a father. But when the time comes, we're gonna figure it out together, okay?"

She nodded, snuggling against his chest.

"In the meantime, we can spend lots of time practicing on the how-to-make-a-baby part."

Rebekah giggled. But she didn't argue.

26

Making love to Rebekah last night had been incredible, and Gregory still wasn't used to the joy of waking up with her beside him in bed. He hoped he'd never get used to it. Every day with her really did feel like a miracle.

"You should come to work with me today," he told her. "You could actually do stuff now. Like, you can eat the food and smell and touch everything." He frowned. "Well, I mean, only if you want to. God knows you've spent so much time in Colonial Williamsburg, I wouldn't blame you if you never wanted to set foot there again."

"No, I would love to go with you. It would be fun to actually be able to experience everything there."

Gregory's eyes lit up. "Hey, I could finally take you to Raleigh Tavern and get you some gingerbread and tea."

"Oh, that sounds wonderful!" Rebekah said, clasping her hands together.

Talk about low maintenance. It's so easy to make her happy.

"If you wear your old dress, you can pass for an

employee again, and you can sing while I play the harpsichord."

"You're right. That's a great idea."

"And now it won't even matter if Ben is at work. I kinda hope he is there. I can't wait to introduce you as my girlfriend to everybody."

Rebekah's eyes lit up with pleasure and pride.

And someday, I'll be able to introduce you as my fiancée. And then as my wife.

∼

THEY HAD a terrific morning at work. Rebekah sang while he played the harpsichord when there were tourists around, and she spent half the time gleefully touching everything in the shop. It was adorable, and Gregory loved seeing her so happy.

They ate lunch, *both* of them, under their usual tree. They needed the shade from the intense summer heat. After that, they started toward Raleigh Tavern for dessert. For Rebekah, anyway. Gregory's blood sugar was a tad too high to indulge in sweets, but he didn't mind. All he really wanted was to watch Rebekah eat and enjoy one of her favorite foods.

As they walked down Duke of Gloucester Street, Rebekah spied Orlando strutting down the road in his usual colonial getup.

"Orlando! Oh, I need to speak with him!" she exclaimed.

"Why?" Gregory asked with suspicion, even a touch of anger, in his voice.

"Gregory," Rebekah admonished. "I'm allowed to speak to other men."

He winced, realizing what an idiot he was being.

"Of course you are. I'm sorry. I guess I'm gonna have to get used to sharing you with the world."

"You sure are. Darling," she said somberly, "except for you, I'm all alone in this world. I'm going to need all the friends I can get."

"You're right." He glanced at Orlando walking toward them and gestured for Rebekah to go ahead and approach him.

She nodded her head sharply in approval and walked over to Orlando. Gregory grinned at her. She might be new to life, but she wasn't about to put up with any nonsense from him. He couldn't help admiring her for it.

"Hey, you're still here," Orlando said, eyes wide when he saw her. Rebekah was wearing her old colonial dress, so he couldn't have noticed anything different about her. He glanced questioningly at Gregory and then back at her.

He suddenly felt terrible for not telling Orlando straight away what had happened with Rebekah. He had always been supportive and concerned for Gregory's welfare. Letting him know she was back to stay had completely slipped his mind.

"The last I heard, you were headed back toward the river where you died," he said, lowering his voice so as not to alarm nearby tourists. "Gregory didn't think you'd be coming back. I'm sorry you're still stuck here, but it sure is nice to see your pretty face."

The compliment made Rebekah smile, and Gregory found it hard to be jealous. She was beautiful and kind, and she deserved to be admired.

"I'm not as stuck as you might think," Rebekah explained. "You see, when I was alive, I was sort of responsible for my little brother's accidental drowning death."

Gregory admired her bravery for telling Orlando what

had happened. He was relieved to hear her finally referring to the tragedy as an accident.

"That's sad," Orlando said, his face full of compassion and devoid of judgment.

"Yeah, it was. I felt so terrible about it that, not long after, I drowned myself in the same river."

"That's *really* sad," Orlando said, still eying her with concern.

Rebekah nodded. "Gregory helped me deal with my emotions and grief, and he helped me understand it was a tragic accident, and that I hadn't meant to hurt my brother."

"Of course you didn't," Orlando said. "You'd never hurt anyone on purpose."

She told him how she had returned to the site of the tragedy and that she had been blessed with a visit from her beloved brother.

"Then, after that, the most incredible thing happened."

Rebekah reached out and squeezed Orlando on the shoulder.

He gasped loudly and took a full step backward.

She laughed heartily. "You look more freaked out now than you did the last time you tried to touch me," she said, her pretty eyes sparkling with amusement.

"B—but h—how ... How it this possible?" he sputtered.

"It's a miracle," Gregory and Rebekah said in perfect unison, as if they'd practiced it. They both laughed, enjoying Orlando's reaction.

"Because my brother and I both died so young, we were supposed to go back and start over. Be born again and have a second chance at life. That's what Nathaniel did. He came back as an infant. Because Gregory and I are in love, I was allowed to come back now, just as I am."

"Wow. I just don't know what else to say," Orlando said, marveling at Rebekah. "Wow."

He reached out and engulfed her in a warm hug.

"So, you're really back? Like, back to stay?" he asked.

Rebekah nodded.

Orlando turned to Gregory. "Dude. Oh my God."

"I know," Gregory said, shaking his head in wonder.

Orlando grabbed him in a warm embrace, too, and then he stepped back to look at them both.

"I could not be more happy for the two of you. Wow, just ... Wow."

"Thanks, man. For everything, you know?" Gregory said, and Orlando clapped him on the back.

"Orlando, before my brother left, he gave me a message for you."

"For me?" he asked, looking perplexed. Then his eyes went wide. "Do you mean from ...

"Yes," Rebekah said softly. "Nathaniel gave me a message for you from your mother."

Orlando froze in place. Then he nodded, ready for her to continue.

"She said 'Don't be stupid, Orlando. Of course I'm proud of you. And I know you feel like it will never happen, but it will. Keep the faith.' Nathaniel said you would know what that means."

"Wow," Orlando said, processing the information. "That sounds like her. It really does. She would say something like that."

"Orlando," Rebekah said gently but firmly. "She *did* say it."

His eyes well with tears. "Thank you," he whispered.

Rebekah put her hand over her heart. "It's my pleasure. Believe me."

Gregory watched Rebekah with admiration. It made her so happy to spread joy to others.

What a wonderful woman she is.

"See ya 'round man," Gregory said, wanting to give Orlando some time alone with his thoughts. "Thanks for everything."

Orlando looked dazed as he walked away.

"Hey, can we stop somewhere first before we go to Raleigh?" Gregory asked.

"Sure. Lead the way," Rebekah said.

He took her by the hand and led her to the front of the Governor's Palace. She eyed the palace curiously.

"Why are we here?"

"This might sound kind of silly, but remember that time we saw the wedding here?"

Rebekah nodded.

"I just remember that day, and how badly I wanted to kiss you in front of the palace. And now I want to do it, since it's actually possible."

She put her hand over her heart like she always did when she was feeling emotional. He loved that sweet gesture of hers.

"It's not silly at all. It's beautiful."

Gregory pulled her close. Smiling down at her, he tenderly cupped her face and kissed her.

This.

This is what true love feels like.

27

Paige Bratton drew in a deep breath, loving the smell of the autumn air in the Colonial Williamsburg historical district. It was a combination of smoke used to cook delicious meats, the fire from the fireplaces, and mulled spices. She enjoyed strolling through the historical areas in the evenings when the crowds had thinned. A Film and Media Studies major at the College of William and Mary, she relished this peaceful time in the evening when she could take a break from her homework and clear her head. Today's classes had been particularly tedious. Though she relished her media and film classes, there were so many boring required ones she had to take, like algebra and biology.

The evening break from school was nice, but it wasn't like quiet time was in short supply at home. Paige lived alone in an apartment off campus. Having taken a few years off after high school, she was older than many of the college students. She had no interest in taking part in the college drinking and partying scene, and she was grateful she could afford to live without a roommate.

As she walked past the Peyton Randolph House, something—or *someone*—grabbed her ankle hard enough to yank her off her feet. She crashed to the ground with a loud cry.

Whipping her head around, she looked for the perpetrator, but there was no one there. It would have been impossible for anyone to grab her like that and run off that quickly without her seeing them.

Panic began to rise in her. Just as her brain formed the thought *My God, what if it was a ghost,* she saw a dark-skinned woman appear before her. The spirit was angry, no doubt about it. The ghostly woman stayed just long enough for Paige to register her existence.

Paige drew in another deep breath. And she screamed.

Soon, she heard pounding footsteps heading straight toward her. Terrorized, Paige struggled to her feet. Quaking with fear, she knew she had to pull it together and run.

"Hey. Hey! Are you all right?" a concerned male voice boomed. She turned to see a man in colonial dress walking toward her.

Despite her terror, Paige's brain managed to register who it was.

Orlando Blake.

Only the most handsome man in all of Colonial Williamsburg. The sexy colonial reenactor she had admired from afar for months. As a future film director, she appreciated fine acting talent. Orlando had terrific stage presence. She especially enjoyed his fiery speeches outside the courthouse. She'd never managed to get the nerve to speak to him, and now, given her terror and nervousness, it would take every ounce of restraint she had not to make a complete fool of herself in front of him.

"Y—yes. I'm all right. I think," she managed to say. Her

knees wobbled from the sheer adrenaline rush, and he grabbed onto her to steady her.

"What happened? Did someone attack you?"

"Yes ... Well, sort of. I think so. You're gonna think I'm crazy ..."

Orlando glanced over at the Peyton Randolph House and then back at her. "Did someone ... someone you didn't see attack you?"

Paige's eyes went wide. "Yes! How did you know?"

"To put it bluntly, this place is haunted. Lemme guess, something grabbed your ankle?"

Her eyes went wide.

"It's okay. It's gonna be okay. Pretty sure that was Jackey."

"Jackey?"

Orlando nodded grimly. "She doesn't like me, either. See?" Orlando pulled up his sock and showed her a bruise on his ankle. Paige gasped.

"It's okay," Orlando said in a gentle voice. "I know it's scary, but that seems to be all she does. Grabs people and scares them."

"She sure did scare me."

"I know. I'm sorry that happened. Can I walk you back to your car or something?" Orlando asked, his gorgeous brown eyes full of concern for her.

"S—sure."

Orlando squeezed her shoulder in support, and Paige walked next to him on shaky legs.

Ghosts were real. Orlando Blake was walking her home.

What a day this had turned out to be.

CONTINUE on with the Williamsburg Ghost Series with Eternal Hope, OR if you are new to the whole Ghost Series thing and you want to read in the official "correct" order – you can see where it all began with the first book in The Gettysburg Ghost Series – Somebody's Darling. The Gettysburg Ghost series is a completed trilogy and takes place before The Williamsburg Ghost series.

SERIES ORDER

The Gettysburg Ghost Series

Somebody's Darling
Darling Soldiers
Forever, Darling

The Williamsburg Ghost Series

Eternal Love
Eternal Hope
Eternal Glory

Made in the USA
Middletown, DE
10 September 2025